Ardent Rising

By Cathleen Ryan

COPYRIGHT

The characters and events in this book are fictitious. Any similarity to real persons, living or dead, is coincidental and not intended by the author.

Partial editing by Jessica Lewis

Cover design and photo by John Leonard

ISBN 9781494334673

TABLE OF CONTENTS

CHAPTER ONE

She could feel the wetness of the light misty rain from above her. The pain had finally subsided from the knife wounds that he had inflicted on her not long before. He then brought her to the last place she would ever be at on this earth. She closed her eyes and slipped into the sleep of death. As her spirit floated out of her body she could see herself lying on the ground, but somehow it no longer mattered as she left this world for the next.

~~~~~~~~~~

It was business as usual for Nikki; a 28 year old veteran police officer who had just arrived for duty when the phone began to ring. She had joined the force at 23, motivated by her unconscious desire to help those who feel helpless to defend themselves. As she picked up the phone and stated, "Officer Ardent," she could feel the hesitation on the other end. "Can I help you?" She inquired.
~~~~~~~~~~

A woman answered, "Yes, my name is Amanda Westlake; I need to report that my roommate didn't come home last night. I think that something may have happened to her."

"Why do you think that something happened?" Nikki questioned.

"She always comes home, and she isn't answering her phone. I'm sure something happened!" She replied in a quiet tone as she struggled to speak the words.

"Can you come to the station and bring a picture of your roommate?"

"Yes, I, I'll be in shortly… will you be there officer Ardent?"

"Just ask for me at the desk, I'll be waiting." As Nikki hung up the phone she suddenly had chills run up and down her arms. As she rubbed her arms to ease the chills she thought to herself, "It's been a long time since that happened, this can't be good."

A first impression of Nikki Ardent would not lead anyone to think she's a police officer. Built slender at 5'6", her dark brown hair hangs to her mid back, it's straight with not a wave or curl. She wears it up so that it will fit under her hat when on the job. Her eyes could pass for those of a doe, large, deep brown, with long eye lashes. Which are only overshadowed by her complexion, a flawless olive, inherited from her mother's Greek ancestry.

"Ardent, hey Ardent, there's someone here for you." Officer James Greene called from the front desk.

"Yea, coming." Nikki called as she rose from her desk and made her way to the front of the station. Weaving around the desks of her co-workers that were filled with piles of manila envelopes, computers, and small tokens that were placed on the edges of the desks in an attempt to individualize their workspace. The office was crowded, each of the officers had a desk. There were two jail cells in the back, two interrogation rooms to the right, and a mutual kitchen and bathroom to the left that was shared with the firemen.

The police station and firehouse occupied the same building that had once been a fairly large home in the center of town. The fire trucks were in a building constructed to hold them and the police cars next to the station. It replaced a home no longer fit for anyone to live in. Being vacant for over a decade with no up keep, the elements had taken their toll. The police and firemen were housed on the first floor of the old home that was renovated to accommodate the two public services. Each was given half of the floor with their own entrance. The second floor housed the court and offices for town business: the town clerk, tax collector, and treasurer.

"Amanda?" Nikki asked.

"Yes, I brought a picture of my roommate Suzy, like you asked."

"Come with me, we can talk in the back." Nikki led Amanda to one of the interrogation rooms so they could talk in private. It was unusual for Nikki to take such an interest in a call from a concerned person that could very well end up being nothing more than Amanda overreacting. Her roommate may have stayed out all night with a date, and her phone battery may have died. After all, a person is not considered missing after a single night. And with no real evidence to suspect foul play Nikki wondered why she was so drawn to hear what Amanda had to say.

Nikki led Amanda to the first interrogation room, "Have a seat here at the table." After Amanda sat down Nikki sat across from her.

Amanda handed Nikki the picture. "This is Suzy; we have been friends for over 10 years."

Nikki looked at the picture of a medium built, light brown haired girl in her early 20's, modestly dressed in a flowered shirt. She wore very little makeup, and was sitting on a large boulder, smiling as if she had not a care in the world."

"Where and when was this photo taken?" Nikki asked.

"It was taken last summer." Tears welling up in her eyes, and her words cracking, Amanda tried to finish her sentence, "We spent a day in the state forest just north of here hiking on the trails."

Nikki excused herself and went to her desk to get a box of tissues for Amanda, when she returned Amanda had composed herself.

"You told me that it was unlike Amanda not to come home, and that she didn't answer her phone. Do you know where she was yesterday?"

"She left early, before I woke up." Sniffling Amanda continued, "She works as a secretary at South Shore Memorial Hospital and has to be there by 7 AM."

"What time does she usually get home?" Nikki asked.

"About 4 o'clock, but I was out with my boyfriend and didn't get home till 10 o'clock. Suzy still wasn't home and didn't come home all night!"

"Is there anything else you can think of that makes you think something happened to her. Maybe something she might have said to you over the last week or so?"

"Not that I can remember." Amanda was calmer now, she had stopped crying.

"I'll tell you what Amanda, I can't put in a report that she is missing right now, and it's too soon for anything to be done officially. But I'll look into this myself, off the record, and see what I can find out. Okay."

"Thank you officer Ardent. I just didn't know what else to do but call the police. I'm not the type of person who jumps to conclusions, or worries at the drop of a hat." Amanda explained.

As Nikki led Amanda to the front of the station, she handed her a pad and asked, "Will you write your phone number and address here, along with Suzy's phone number?"

"Yes, of course." Amanda readily agreed. As she wrote, Nikki could see that her hands were slightly shaking. Having just met this woman, Nikki wondered how hard a hat had to drop to make her worry.

Amanda handed Nikki the pad, thanked her again and headed out of the station.

Returning to her desk, Nikki took a deep breath, as she sat staring at the phone numbers on the pad, and then the picture of Suzy. She felt herself drawn to the picture, and wondered if this vibrant young woman was still breathing. And then wondered why she even thought that, and how morbid she was becoming these days.

She pushed back from her desk, picked up her keys and called to her partner, Jim Hershen, who was sitting at the desk behind hers. "I need to go check on something, do you want to come?"

"Sure, kiddo, I need a break. Where are we going?"

Jim was 37; he joined the force after serving in the army for 10 years. His wife's name was Laura and they have 2 sons. He had 9 years on the job, when his first partner retired. When Nikki arrived they were paired up and have been working together ever since.

"I just want to check something out, ease my mind." Nikki explained.

Once in the car Nikki told Jim the events of the morning as they drove to South Shore Memorial Hospital. The drive from the station to the hospital was no more than 15 minutes. The hospital was located near the lake on the outskirts of town. It was a two story building housing an emergency room, 2 medical floors, an intensive care unit, and an operating room.

Nikki and Jim went to the desk at the main entrance to get directions to the personnel office to inquire about Suzy.

"Can I help you?" A woman in her 50's came from a room off to the side of the personnel office.

"Yes, I'm Officer Ardent and this is Officer Hershen. We had a few questions about Suzy Lamoy. I understand she works here."

"She does, but she didn't show up for work this morning. We called her cell phone but she didn't answer." The woman stated.

Nikki and Jim gave each other a glance, both understanding what the other was thinking.

"Has she done this before?" Nikki questioned.

"No, I don't believe so. Is she alright?"

"That's what we're trying to find out. Is there anyone here who is close with her we can talk to?"

"Hold on a second." The woman said as she went back to her desk.

Nikki and Jim could hear her on the phone. "Hi Terry, could you send Kadi and Cindy to my office?" She returned after hanging up, "Cindy and Kadi spend time with Suzy, they eat lunch and take breaks together. They may be able to help you."

Waiting silently until the two girls arrived, Nikki couldn't help but think the worst, and wondered if either of the girls would be able to give them a lead.

Within minutes the door next to them began to open and two girls in their early twenties came into the room. They both glanced at the police officers with some confusion and then to the woman who had called them. "These officers are here to ask you about Suzy. Why don't you go back here into my office where you can have some privacy?" She said as she pointed toward her office door.

The two girls entered the room followed by Nikki and Jim. Nikki motioned to the girls, "Please take a seat." Once the girls sat Nikki continued, "Did you two work with Suzy yesterday?"

"Yes." They answered in unison.

"Can you tell me where she was going after work last night?"

Kadi spoke first, "I don't recall her saying she was doing anything."

Cindy, hesitating spoke up. "I heard her on her phone, she told someone she would see them in a half hour. I didn't ask her about it. I'm sorry, is she alright?"

"That's what we're trying to find out." Nikki replied.

Jim asked, "Do you know what kind of car she drives?"

"It's a small silver car." Cindy said. "I don't know what kind; she bought it a year ago at the car dealer in Middletown."

"Thank you. If either of you think of anything else please call the station." Jim said as he and Nikki excused themselves and left the hospital to go to their vehicle.

"This doesn't look good, does it?" Nikki remarked as she fastened her seat belt. "Let's go back to the station and start working this."

“Looks like something may have happened to this girl after all. I guess her roommate was right coming to you this morning.” Jim said.

“Yeah.” Is all Nikki could answer; she had a lump in the pit of her stomach. It was almost eight years ago now that her best friend had gone missing, she vanished one evening on her way home from work. Not a trace was ever found. Two years later Nikki joined the police force.

When they arrived at the station Nikki and Jim began to put into motion all the necessary elements to try and find Suzy Lamoy. They spoke with their Captain, Larry Spruce, who agreed that this was a case that needed immediate attention. He took the picture Amanda had given Nikki and gave copies to the other officers in the station. He also sent a fax to the police stations in the surrounding towns so they could aid in the search as well.

Jim contacted Suzy’s parents to see if they had seen her, or if they might have some idea who it was she was speaking to on the phone when she left work. He also wanted to see if they knew the make, model and year of her car.

Nikki called Amanda, Suzy's roommate, to see if she could help them with the same information.

Nikki and Jim reported back to their captain with the information from their phone calls.

Nikki began by stating that Amanda believed Suzy drove a silver Hyundai Elantra, but didn't know the year. She had no idea who it was Suzy could have been talking to on the phone.

Jim's conversation with Suzy's parents yielded the same information with the addition of her father knowing that her car was a 2000. They were both on their way to the station, along with Suzy's sister who was a senior in high school. Jim had tried to persuade them to stay at home and that they would contact them if anything new arose, but they insisted.

"Jim." Frank called, there's someone here for you.

Jim and Nikki went to the desk to greet Suzy's parents; Marshall and Joanne, along with her sister Penny. "Let's go where it's more private." Jim said as he took the lead and guided them to the first interrogation room. "Have a seat, Nikki and I will do our best to explain the situation."

Jim motioned to Nikki to begin the conversation. "Amanda called this morning because she was worried about Suzy. She didn't come home last night, and she didn't show up for work this morning either. She had made a phone call to someone before she left work yesterday and was going to meet them. This is all we really know right now, is there anything you can add?" Nikki asked.

Marshall and Joanne were visibly upset over the thought of their oldest daughter being missing. Nikki wanted to somehow take the feelings of panic and anguish from them but knew it wasn't possible. Only finding Suzy alive and well would make that possible, and with the way things looked that seemed an unlikely end to this case.

Nikki glanced at Penny who was sitting quiet and unmoved, clutching her small purse in her lap. "When did you see or speak with your sister last Penny?"

Penny burst into tears, speaking words that were barely audible, "I was the one she spoke with from work yesterday, she was supposed to meet me and never showed up. I thought she was mad at me." Joanne reached over and hugged her youngest daughter.

"Where was she supposed to meet you?" Nikki asked after Penny began to calm down.

Regaining her composure Penny replied. "At the lake, by the picnic tables. I was late and I thought she was upset with me and left before I got there."

"What on earth is going on Penny, why would Suzy be upset with you for that?" Her mother asked.

"I can't, mom, not now." Penny replied, shrinking into her chair wanting to just disappear.

Marshall, who was silent until now stood up. “Penny, why would Suzy be mad at you for being late, that doesn’t make sense.”

“Dad, I…” Marshall interrupted his youngest daughter. “No. I want an explanation, your sister is missing!”

“I know, I know.” It was obvious Penny did not want to speak the words that needed to be said. She put her hand over her face, and tilted her head down as she spoke. “I think I’m pregnant, okay. Suzy was going to go with me to buy a pregnancy test from the drug store.” Penny burst into tears again, her mother reached for her to hug and comfort her. Marshall sat back down, placing one hand on Penny’s back and the other on his wife’s shoulder as Penny and her mother both sobbed in each other’s arms.

Nikki and Jim left the room to give the family time alone. “When things calm down in there we need to find out who Penny has been seeing. Maybe Suzy went to find him when Penny wasn’t at the lake. It’s a long shot but I don’t want to overlook anything.” Nikki remarked to Jim.

Jim excused himself and went to the captain to ask him to have a patrol car go to the lake and look around. He and Nikki would remain at the station to continue their interview with Suzy's family.

After a few minutes Nikki knocked on the door of the interrogation room and popped her head in the door. "Are you okay in there?"

"Yes." Marshall answered, "Come in."

Motioning to Jim who was over by the captain's door, Nikki returned to the Lamoy family with Jim entering the room shortly after. Marshall had returned to his seat next to Joanne who was still sitting with her arm around her youngest daughter. Penny was still a little teary but otherwise calm. "We only have one more question for now. Penny, what is your boyfriend's name?"

"It's Sam, Sam Archibald." Penny slowly replied looking down at her lap, not wanting to look up and face anyone.

"He lives on Merchant Street, in the green house with the white shutters." Joanne added.

Nikki and Jim thanked the Lamoys for coming in and promised to keep them posted with any developments. Jim led the family to the front door of the station and opened the door for them as they walked out.

Marshall leaned over to Jim as he passed him, "Do you think Sam is involved in Suzy's disappearance?"

"We just like to have a complete picture of what's going on, we have no reason to suspect him of anything." Jim tried to assure Marshall who shook his head acknowledging he understood as he turned to catch up to his family.

Returning to his desk Jim saw Nikki sitting with her head in her hands, leaning on her desk with her elbows. She sensed Jim behind her and turned around.

"This case brings back memories of Stacey, deep down I feel there's a connection between her disappearance and Suzy's. How can that even be possible Jim?" Nikki looked to him for an answer even though she knew he wouldn't have one for her question.

"Well kiddo, if there is we'll find it, now let's go talk to Sam Archibald to see if he has anything that can help us."

"Jim, Nikki!" The captain called from his office door. "Get over to the hospital, they think that missing girl's car might be in the parking lot."

To Nikki it seemed as though they would never get to the hospital, she sat in the passenger seat of the squad car silent as Jim drove. She was thinking about Suzy, wondering how they would ever find her. In this small town no one disappears, there hadn't been a murder since Nikki joined the force. The last one was over 10 years ago and that happened during a fight at the town bar, it was ruled an accident. Nikki could see the crowd in the parking lot as they came around to the entrance, "That must be the place." She said pointing at the crowd.

Jim parked the squad car behind what appeared to be Suzy's car. He and Nikki got out and walked over to the crowd. "Excuse us!" Jim announced, "Can everyone step back so we can check the car out please!"

The dozen employees who had heard that Suzy was missing and that her car was still in the parking lot were waiting for answers. They were curious and concerned at the same time.

The security guard who had discovered the car spoke up. “Officers, my name is Gerry Thiemann, I noticed the car while I was making my rounds.”

“Has anyone opened the doors or entered the car?” Nikki asked, as she put on a pair of vinyl gloves.

“No, I’ve been with the car waiting for you to get here.” The security guard replied.

As Nikki and Jim looked in the car, Nikki noticed a purse between the seats. As she pulled on the door handle she held her breath, if it was open it wouldn’t be a good sign. It was. “Jim, nobody leaves their purse in a car, especially an unlocked one!”

Jim attempted to open the passenger side door, it too was unlocked. He looked in the back seat and saw nothing of any use.

Nikki picked up Suzy's purse, her wallet and other items were inside. The purse looked as though it had been hastily tossed in the car, it was tipped onto its side with her brush half out.

"Do you see her keys anywhere Jim?"

Jim searched under the seat, and in the cushion on the passenger side with no luck. "No, I don't Nikki; she must have used them to open the door if it was locked."

Nikki looked around on her side of the car, and then bent down to look underneath the car. She laid on her side to reach under farther and pulled out a set of keys. Placing the key in the door lock she took a breath and closed her eyes as she turned it, the door locked, and opened with a second turn. She looked at Jim who was looking back.

The tow truck arrived to tow the car to the police lot. Nikki gathered Suzy's purse and keys, then placed them in a plastic bag to take with her and Jim back to the station.

Once in their squad car Nikki radioed ahead to the captain and filled him in on what they had found.

“This is getting too big for us, I’m going to call the state police and get some help down here.” Captain Spruce explained. “I don’t like where this is headed.”

“Okay captain, Jim and I agree, we don’t like this either, see you in a few minutes.”

“We really have no idea where this girl could be, where do we go from here? I have never felt as clueless in an investigation as I do with this one. Who in our town would take a young woman; it must be someone who’s not from here.” Jim remarked.

“That’s our next lead Jim, looking for someone that is new or not from here! And you’re probably right, who in this town would be capable of doing this?”

CHAPTER TWO

It was a warm afternoon in the Adirondacks, Jill and Mary had decided to take a hike on the trails of the state forest. The hilly trails were beautiful this time of year. The leaves on each type of tree were a different shade of green, the birds sang their individual songs, and a chattering squirrel could be heard voicing his displeasure at the two women who entered his woods. The creek that ran next to the trail they were hiking babbled as it flowed over the rocks and pebbles that lined it. It was one of the first warm spring days of the year, and all of nature seemed to be rejoicing with its appearance.

The two women, in their mid-thirties, had taken up hiking to stay fit. They usually walked in town but with such a nice day decided they would stretch their wings and try something a little more challenging. When they reached the top of the large hill they were climbing they felt it was a good spot to eat the dinner they had packed. They were sitting on large boulders enjoying their meal, talking and laughing when Jill spotted something.

“Look Mary, is that someone walking down there?” She pointed behind Mary, down the hill on the other side of the valley. Mary turned to look but couldn’t see what Jill was pointing to.

“There is someone there, he just went behind a patch of trees, and it looked like he was carrying something.” Jill explained.

The two women sat looking toward the spot where Jill had seen the figure go behind the trees. As he emerged the two women pointed and exclaimed, “There he is!” In unison.

“He doesn’t seem to be carrying anything, are you sure he had something Jill?”

“I thought so; it looked like a sleeping bag. What would someone be doing there, there aren’t any trails on that side of the valley and no one lives near here.”

“I don’t know, but we should start back. I don’t want to be out here when it starts getting dark.” Mary said as she picked up the remains of her dinner and put it in her back pack.

Jill watched as the man slowly walked back the way he came until she couldn't see him any longer. "Yea, your right Mary we do need to head back so we don't have to rush down the trail."

The two women started down the hill on their way back toward town. Mary didn't give any more thought to the person they had seen, but Jill couldn't stop thinking about the encounter. It seemed out of the ordinary to her that anyone would be on that side of the valley.

~ ~ ~ ~ ~ ~ ~ ~ ~ ~

On Saturday evening Jill's husband Harry was having the weekly poker game at their house, he and the five other men who met weekly for a tournament rotated who would host the game. They had a twenty dollar buy in and the winner left with the one hundred and twenty dollar jackpot.

Lester Snell, a 50 year old conservation police officer was at the poker game. Remembering what he did for a living Jill decided she would speak to him about the man in the forest. During a break in the poker tournament she brought out fresh drinks and chips for their guests and saw Lester standing over by the front window. “Hi Lester, how is your wife doing?” Jill asked to open the conversation.

“She’s recuperating from the surgery, having her knee replaced was the best thing she could have done. She hasn’t had any pain in a few weeks. I’ll tell her you asked about her.”

“Thanks Les. I’ve always enjoyed seeing her at the church fundraisers. It hasn’t been quite the same without her. By the way, I was hiking on the Sky View Trail with Mary last Thursday. We made it to the top and saw a man over on the other side of the valley. He carried something behind a patch of trees and a few minutes later left without it. I didn’t know that anyone was over that way. Do you know who it could have been?”

“I’ll go have a look Monday when I’m on duty. Nobody should be there though, the only time anyone would ever go there might be during hunting season. There’s some rough terrain on that side of the valley, anyone over there must have had a specific reason for being there.”

“It seemed suspicious to me.” Jill continued. “Whatever he carried in, he left there. It looked like a sleeping bag or sack of some sort. Do you think he is homeless and is living there?”

“I doubt it, getting in and out is tough. There are a lot more places with easier access for someone to set up a camp.”

“Les, hey Les, we’re starting back up.” Harry called.

“Okay, be right over. I’ll go take a look Jill. I’ll let you know if I find anything.”

“Thank you, Les.” Feeling reassured now that Les was involved, Jill went to the kitchen to clean the dishes that had accumulated during the day before heading off to bed.

~ ~ ~ ~ ~ ~ ~ ~ ~ ~ ~

Monday morning came around quickly. As he drove to the ranger barracks Les thought how weekdays seemed to go by much slower than the weekends. “It should be the other way around.” He said to himself as he pulled into the parking lot.

When he entered the log cabin style barracks, nestled among a dozen tall pine trees on the outskirts of the state forest, he could smell freshly brewed coffee.

“Good morning Les. Are you ready for another week?” David, the second of three conservation police that patrolled the Southern Adirondack State Park and surrounding woodlands, sarcastically remarked.

“Not much of a choice now is there.” Remarked Les who was looking forward to his retirement in 5 years, when he would be able to collect his full pension. He had been on the job for twenty-five years and was getting too old to be traipsing throughout God’s Country much longer.

“Did Luther get in yet?” Les asked David as he poured himself a cup of black coffee.

“Not yet.”

“When he does I need one of you to come with me to check out a possible squatter across from the Sky View Trail rest area.”

"I'll go with you; we can take Caesar. He could use a good run." Caesar was the two year old German shepherd that lived at the barracks. He was a search and rescue dog that would help find the half dozen or so hikers who would come up from the city and leave the forest trails in search of an adventure. Even though they could find their own way out if they walked in a straight line in any direction for two miles or so, one out of ten would get lost and need to be found before a bear or the elements got to them first.

Les and David sat reliving their weekend off when Luther pulled up in his pickup truck. David called Caesar over and put his leash on while Les met Luther at the door and explained where he and David were going. They each grabbed a walkie-talkie, since there was no cell service in many parts of the park, water canteens, and finally armed themselves with their pistols before starting out the door.

Les knew the forest like the back of his hand. He thought it a stretch that anyone would choose to set up a camp in that part of the forest. It was rugged, not many hunters even ventured into that area, but it was his duty to check out the circumstances.

As they came out from the tree line into the field that was below the rest area, David let Caesar off his leash to run around in the open field.

Looking up Les pointed to the rest area above. “There’s the spot Jill said they looked down from.”

The two men looked around. “It might be those trees over there she was talking about. It’s a good place to start anyway.” David remarked pointing at a group of white birch trees.

As they walked toward the group of trees Caesar began to bark, they recognized the tone. “He found someone!” David exclaimed.

“Maybe it’s our squatter.” Les remarked as they ran toward Caesar’s bark.

As they came near the trees they stopped as if on cue. Looked at each other, and slowly walked toward the spot the odor was coming from. Caesar was sitting in the middle of the birch trees. He turned when he heard the footsteps of Les and David, as he turned he whined and then looked back in the direction he had been barking in.

Lying there in the middle of the trees was the body of a young woman, fully clothed, her face easily recognizable as Suzy Lamoy!

CHAPTER THREE

"Captain Spruce?" Asked the voice on the other end of the phone.

"Yes, speaking, can I help you?"

"I'm returning your call. I received a message that you contacted the missing persons division of the State Police Troop D on Friday evening to report a missing woman." Trooper Sean Riley replied.

"We have a situation that we feel requires a little more expertise than we have here." The captain explained the details to the state trooper.

"I think you're right, you definitely could use some help with this. We'll see you in a couple of hours." Trooper Riley replied as he hung up the phone on his end.

Captain Spruce sat at his desk for a few seconds holding the phone to his ear, relieved that the State Police Investigation Team was coming. He wanted to do all he could to find this poor woman.

After hanging up the phone he left his office and went to the break room where Nikki was getting a cup of coffee. "Ardent good news, the troopers will be here soon to help us look for Suzy Lamoy."

"I'm really glad to hear that captain. Jim and I were talking on the way back from the hospital on Friday, we don't think anyone local is involved with this. It must be someone who is new here or was passing through. We also stopped by Sam Archibald's house but he wasn't home, we're going to go back when Jim gets here."

"Good, I'll be getting everything together for when the troopers arrive." Seeing Jim walk across the room Captain Spruce pointed saying, "Looks like Jim's here now, let me know what you two find."

"Okay captain." Nikki was holding a cup of coffee in each hand as she left the break room. "Here you go partner, we don't have time to sit and chat, troopers are on their way. I want to go talk to Sam so we can get back before they get here."

"Nice cup of coffee!" Jim remarked taking a sip of the fresh coffee Nikki had brewed as they walked from the station to their patrol car.

When they arrived at Sam Archibald's home Nikki noticed someone leaving the back yard out the side gate. "Go around to the side street Jim, I think I saw Sam go that way."

As they came around the corner Sam saw the car and started running down the street, "What in the world is he doing?" Remarked Jim as he drove after him.

"Stop at the corner. We'll be close enough for me to get him there." At the corner Nikki jumped out of the car to chase Sam across the lawns of the adjacent neighborhood. Sam was starting to tire and Nikki had no problems catching up to him. "Stop, Sam, we want to talk to you."

Realizing his effort to get away from the officers was useless as he heard Nikki behind him and saw the police car keeping pace with him on the street, Sam stopped.

"Why did you try to run from us Sam? You obviously saw us from inside as we pulled up to your house." Nikki questioned.

Jim had pulled the car to the side of the road and joined Nikki. "Do we need to take you down to the station? What has gotten into you?" Jim yelled as he approached the young man.

"I thought you were going to arrest me." Sam said looking at the officers with fear in his eyes.

"Arrest you for what?" Nikki asked.

Sam was hesitant about answering.

Jim didn't want to prolong the conversation in front of the neighborhood so he moved closer to Sam and put his arm around his shoulder. "Let's go take a ride Sam, people are starting to stare at us."

"Okay, I'm sorry. I'm just freaked out after talking to Penny's dad last night."

After they had gotten into the car and started to drive back to Sam's house Jim started the conversation, "What did Mr. Lamoy say to you that freaked you out Sam?"

"He came outside when I was dropping Penny off and said that he knew that Penny was pregnant, and that because she was seventeen when she got pregnant he was going to have me arrested for statutory rape. I thought that was why you were coming to my house."

Jim and Nikki just looked at one another. "No Sam," Nikki continued the conversation. "We were there to see if you saw Suzy at all last Thursday."

"Oh, ah no, I don't remember the last time I saw her, it was maybe two weeks ago."

"Is there anything that you have thought of since you heard she's been missing that might help us? Anything no matter how little or irrelevant it seems that might have popped into your mind?"

"All I can think about is Penny; she is so upset over all this. I don't think there is anything I've seen or heard about Suzy other than what Penny has said."

Jim pulled into Sam's driveway, his mother came out the door and watched as Sam got out of the car and walked over to her. They were talking as Jim backed out of the driveway to head back to the station.

As they pulled in front of the station a state trooper car pulled in a few spaces down. “Just in time.” Jim pointed out the car to Nikki.

Jim and Nikki walked over to the troopers. Jim put his hand out to shake the hand of Trooper Riley. “Hello, I’m Jim Hershen and this is Nikki Ardent. You must be here because of Suzy Lamoy, the young woman that went missing.”

“Hello, yes we are, I’m Sean Riley and this is Wayne Kemph.” Trooper Riley stated as he shook Jim and then Nikki’s hand, followed by Trooper Kemph.

“Let’s head into the station, the captain is waiting.” Leading the way to the door and opening it for the troopers and Nikki, Jim entered last as Nikki led the way to the captain’s office.

Captain Spruce saw them coming as they passed through the gate at the front desk. He rose from his chair and walked over to meet them half way. Nikki immediately knew something was wrong by the captain’s demeanor.

“Have you heard something?” She inquired, not sure if she really wanted to know.

“Let’s go into my office.” Once in the office Captain Spruce shut the door. With his right hand he wiped over the lower half of his face, a habit Nikki recognized from previous encounters with him. He was uncomfortable with what he was about to say.

“I received a call from the conservation police about fifteen minutes ago. They found a body in the state forest. It sounds like it could be our girl. David Morgan is waiting for you at the barracks to escort you to where they found her.”

When they arrived at the barracks David was waiting, he looked a little pale to Nikki as they walked over to him. “She’s in a part of the forest not well trodden; there are no clear paths so no one should lag behind.” David remarked in a monotone businesslike manner as he led them into the forest.

Making their way through the rocky, thick treed woods, David, Nikki, Jim and the troopers came out into the clearing. Ahead of them they could see a patch of white birch trees with multiple figures moving around.

"Les!" Jim called.

"Over here!" A figure was waving his arm and began heading toward them.

"Hey Les, these are Troopers Riley and Kemph from the Bureau of Criminal Investigation (BCI) they came over to help us with the case."

"How did you find the body?" Asked Trooper Riley.

Les explained the tip he received from Jill Mayfield as the reason that they were looking in this particular area.

"The perpetrator must know these woods in order to find his way in here and back out." Trooper Kemph remarked.

"This area is remote and pretty rugged. I suspect it isn't a spot that gets much activity. That could be why he chose it." Added Trooper Riley.

Caesar, who had been sniffing around the area, began barking. Les's face seemed to become ashen as he turned toward the sound of the bark. "That's the bark he makes when he finds someone he's been looking for, the bark he made when he found the body."

The men and Nikki ran toward the dog's bark. It was coming from the other side of the clearing behind the tree line. The pine trees at the edge of the clearing were forty feet tall, their needled branches came to the ground creating a cave like area beneath them.

A wall formed by the branches blocked their view, going between the branches they entered into another world. The ground was covered in old pine needles with nothing growing due to the lack of sun light. The way the branches cascaded down from about five feet up the tree, allowed them to move about fairly easily even though they had to bend at the waist.

"Caesar, here boy." Les called. Caesar whined from behind the trunk of the tree that was in front of where they were standing. As they pushed through the pine covered branches Caesar could be seen sitting next to a bundle of blankets. Les approached and patted Caesar on the head, “Good boy.” He then took a closer look at the partially rotted blanket; using a stick he gently lifted the looser end exposing a skeleton. Standing behind him Nikki, Jim and the troopers could also see what Caesar had found.

CHAPTER FOUR

Standing in front of the bathroom sink, he splashed warm water on his face to remove the cream left behind after shaving. As he began to dry himself off, he glanced in the mirror and then stood looking at himself. "Who are you?" He asked out loud. He stood staring at his own face and yet felt as though he was looking into the eyes of someone he had never met.

After a few seconds he turned and continued getting ready. He smelled the coffee he had started to brew before showering, and was looking forward to that first cup that always seemed to taste better than at any other time during the day.

As he sat sipping his morning cup of coffee he took out his cell phone and pushed six to dial home. "Hi, I'll be leaving here in a few minutes and should be home by noon. Everything went well here, we closed the land deal." … "Yea, I'm glad it is finished too. Do you need anything?" … "Alright, I love you, bye."

He took one last look around the room before leaving to be sure he didn't forget anything. He then walked to the motel's front desk to check out.

"Good morning sir, did you enjoy your stay with us?" The desk clerk asked.

"Everything was fine, thank you." The man said as he finalized his bill and left for his vehicle. It was an SUV, a company car that he used as he sought out properties that could be bought and used for building lots. He worked for the same company for over fifteen years and travelled frequently. As he headed downstate toward the Pennsylvania border he felt content, and relaxed. He went from radio station to radio station by pushing the scan button until he found something of interest.

He had a successful two weeks and he knew that his time in New York was over for now. He looked forward to his next adventure and what it may lead to, but first he was going to head home to Pennsylvania to spend time with his wife. She had been his best friend since they were teenagers. They grew up in the same mining town and she stood by him through the dark days after his father had thrown him out of his house. His family didn't understand him and when he started to have trouble with the local police they couldn't deal with him any longer.

She understood him, possibly because of the abusive home life she had endured with an alcoholic father and a mother who suffered from depression.

They had the same goals in life, neither wanted children, all they wanted was to quietly live their lives. So far they had achieved that. They lived on an old Pennsylvania farm with enough land not to even see another house. They had very little contact with anyone. His job allowed him to stay in contact with his company via phone, fax and email. She was disabled from an injury she received in a car accident when she was eighteen. Her father was driving after drinking too much and crashed into another car, not seeing the stop sign. The crash left her with severe leg injuries, along with a crushed ankle and foot that over a half dozen surgeries could not fix. She now collected disability payments monthly since she was unable to work.

After she had recovered from her surgery they moved in together. He started to work as a carpenter's assistant to support her. Then he eventually fell into the job he had now. They married two years later and have been together for seventeen years.

When he was away she kept busy with housework, a garden, and a flock of chickens that she loved to watch as they chased butterflies across the grass and scratched in the ground for grubs and other insects. They were living their dream.

~ ~ ~ ~ ~ ~ ~ ~ ~ ~ ~

Having vacated the state forest to allow a forensic team to come in and process the area, the officers and troopers headed back to the station in order to continue the investigation.

The other four members of the BCI team had arrived before they returned. They set up one of the interrogation rooms for the briefings they would need to conduct, with the help of Captain Spruce and Officer Bronk.

Standing at the front of the makeshift briefing room, Troopers Riley and Kemph were heading up the conversation concerning the events that had transpired. Raising her hand Nikki waited for Sean Riley, who was the lead on the case, to acknowledge her. She was not convinced that the direction the discussion was going was the right one.

"Officer Ardent, do you want to add something?"

"I don't mean any disrespect, but I really don't believe the killer is from here. I agree that whoever it is must be familiar with the area though."

"How much experience do you have Miss Ardent to even make a statement like that? We have solved quite a few murders. I think we know what we're doing!" Trooper Greene blurted out in response to Nikki's statement.

Nikki stared blankly at the trooper, not quite sure how she should respond to such an obvious attack aimed personally toward her.

"Trooper Greene!" Sean Riley spoke up before Nikki had a chance to reply. "Let's not suppress anyone's opinion. The important thing is to catch this guy."

Nikki was not new to being the subject of ridicule; she had been a target many times during her life. She had developed a tough exterior when it came to this type of abuse. However she was still caught off guard when she didn't expect it.

"Sorry, Sean." Trooper Greene apologized for his outburst.

"Let's continue where we left off. Officer Ardent can you add to your statement please." Riley wanted to put aside the outburst and continue on with the briefing.

The fact that Harry Greene did not apologize to her did not escape Nikki, but she chose to ignore the situation and the comment.
"What I mean is that this is a small town. We know everyone here and have no reason to suspect anyone of harming Suzy, let alone being responsible for more than one murder."

"I agree. There is not a name that even comes to mind!" Jim added in support of his partner.

"I know where you both are coming from." Trooper Kemph remarked. "Just remember the stories of some of the most notorious killers of recent memory. They lived and worked in their communities, some had families, and no one ever suspected them."

"You're right. I'll keep an open mind." Nikki answered feeling as if she would be taking on the six troopers who made up the BCI Unit if she pushed her opinion any further. She chose to go with the flow for now, even though she still did not believe it was anyone local.

"I've been looking over the material that has been collected since Suzy Lamoy went missing until this afternoon. The only person so far without a definite time line is Suzy's sister's boyfriend, Sam Archibald. Nikki and Jim did you ever get to speak with him?" Enquired Trooper Riley.

Jim wanted to give Nikki a reprieve. Putting his hand on her right shoulder to communicate he had this one; he made his way a few steps past her and stopped as he began to speak. "First thing this morning Nikki and I spoke with him by his house. He hadn't seen Suzy for over a week."

“Did he say where he was at the time Suzy was taken?” Trooper Bleaker asked.

“We didn’t directly ask that, he said he hadn’t seen her and we felt that was enough. There is no reason to suspect him; he has no history of trouble.” Jim added.

“You’re probably right but we need to have all of our i’s dotted and t’s crossed. Hines and West go ask him where he was so we have all the pieces to look at.” Trooper Riley directed.

Heading toward the back of the room Jim looked toward Nikki who glanced up as he walked by. They both felt over shadowed by the six troopers on the BCI Team.

“Jim and Nikki, we have the camera footage from the hospital parking lots. Why don’t you two look it over since you’re familiar with the locals and might more easily recognize someone out of place.”

Nikki and Jim nodded their heads in agreement as Trooper Riley continued to assign jobs to everyone at the briefing.

"When we get the autopsy and crime scene results we'll regroup, until then report in when you find anything. Let's go everyone!" Sean Riley began to collect the papers on his temporary desk when Nikki approached him.

"Sir, do you have a minute?"

Sean looked for a second, unconsciously scanning her to determine her motive. "Sure Nikki, what can I do for you?"

"Nikki?" Jim interrupted. He knew what Nikki was about to do and didn't want her to put herself out on a limb she may not be able to get back from.

"It's okay Jim." Nikki turned back toward Trooper Riley. "I wanted to talk to you about something that has been bothering me since this case started. I had a friend, my best friend actually, she disappeared when she was twenty, which is close to eight years ago now. Anyway, I think this case is connected to her disappearance. It's just a gut feeling, I know it seems unrealistic, but I have to put it on the table."

"Get me the records and I'll have a look." Trooper Riley replied without hesitation.

As Nikki and Jim where heading out of the briefing room, Sean walked from behind the desk to the front and called after her. "I appreciate you trusting me enough to share your thoughts Nikki." He said as he leaned against the front of the desk.

Glancing back and smiling Nikki answered. "No problem."

Once they reached their desks Jim realized he was hungry. "Let's order lunch and watch the footage while we eat to save time. What would you like?"

"Pizza, with extra cheese sounds good. If you agree, I'll call and have it delivered." Nikki replied.

"That does sound good. I haven't had John's pizza in quite awhile."

As they sat looking at the video from the hospital parking lot, the delivery boy came with their pizza. They paused the video and practically tore into the pizza box. As they began eating the pizza they realized it may have been more enjoyable if it were not for the reality of the moment. “We’re coming up to three o’clock. Suzy should be coming out to her car shortly.” Nikki remarked watching the time stamp in the lower right corner.

“I know that’s her car, the time stamp says five o’clock now and she hasn’t been near the car. That is the right car isn’t it? Is the time stamp correct?” Thinking out loud, Nikki knew Jim didn’t have an answer.

Pushing the pause button to the video, Nikki stood up running her fingers through the hair on the top of her head, frustrated as she looked toward the floor. “What is going on here Jim? The theory was that Suzy left work and was taken from her car before she could meet with her sister. Now it’s obvious that didn’t happen. Was she taken somewhere between leaving the locker room and getting to her car? Or did she plan on meeting her sister without the use of her car?”

“Let’s keep looking, her purse and keys got there somehow. Maybe we’ll see something at some point. We can also verify the time stamp to be sure it's accurate. I'll call over to the hospital and get that started. Why don't you put on a fresh pot of coffee while I make the call? You make it much better than I do." Jim needed a break and thought Nikki could also use one.

Hearing activity in the station Nikki poked her head out of the break room. Troopers Hines and West had returned and brought Sam with them. The teen looked terrified as the troopers took him into the remaining interrogation room.

Nikki walked over to see what was going on. Hines was talking to Riley. "The kid is hiding something." She heard him telling Sean Riley as she passed the door. She went to the adjacent room where she could see Sam through the one way glass. He was sitting in the chair with his hands on the table, fidgeting around, he was obviously nervous. Nikki left the room to see what more she could find out, being naturally curious was in her nature, and also came with the territory of her job.

Jim had finished his call to the hospital security office and also came over to see what the bustle of activity was about.

“Sam Archibald is in the interrogation room.” Nikki filled Jim in.

Captain Spruce and Trooper Riley headed into the adjacent room while West and Hines went in to speak with Sam. Nikki and Jim followed the captain and stood behind to keep a low profile since they had cleared Sam of wrong doing and now here he was under suspicion by the troopers.

Captain Spruce told Riley how Penny thought she was pregnant and that Sam was the father. That most likely his actions here could have something to do with that. Riley shook his head acknowledging that he heard and understood what the captain was saying.

“Sam, why are you so nervous. Is there something you want to tell us?” Asked Trooper Hines.

“No, I don’t know why you brought me here. I told you and the police that I hadn’t seen Suzy for about a week and a half, and I certainly didn’t kidnap her!”

“Nobody mentioned kidnapping, why would you use that word Sam?” Asked Trooper West.

“That’s what the whole town is saying, that she has been kidnapped by someone. What else would you call it?”

“How about murder!” Trooper Hines said to see his reaction.

“What?” Shocked by the word Sam continued. “No one thinks she’s dead, why would you say that?” Appearing even more scared Sam sat quietly. He wasn’t stupid and realized this was becoming more than he could handle. He didn’t want to talk to them by himself any longer. “I want my parents.”

“Sorry, you’re an adult Sam, you’re over eighteen.” Trooper West stated the fact Sam was not yet accustomed to hearing, only being an adult for the last six months.

“Then I want a lawyer! I don’t know why you even brought me in here!” From watching TV Sam knew that if he asked for a lawyer they couldn’t ask him anything else until he had one, or at least that is what he hoped.

The troopers however looked at the scene differently. To them Sam appeared to be experienced in the ways of the law, which added even more suspicion on their part.

"He's just a scared kid, Riley, just bring his parents in, he'll probably cooperate and answer your questions with them here." Captain Spruce demanded in a respectful way that didn't cause any harsh feelings from Riley.

"Okay, Larry. Go and call them to come in."

Troopers Hines and West walked into the room having ended their conversation with Sam. "He wants his lawyer, seems like he's been down this road before after all." Sarcastically remarked Hines.

"Captain Spruce is going to call his parents to come in…"

Harry Greene, who had returned from speaking to Suzy's roommate and family letting them know that the BCI was working with the local police, interrupted Riley before he could finish. "What do you mean; the kid is clearly guilty of something."

"As I was saying, Captain Spruce is going to call his parents to come in so we can find out what is going on with him." Sean Riley continued, ignoring Greene.

Captain Spruce returned from his office after speaking to Sam's father. "They'll be here in ten minutes."

"While we're waiting, Harry, come and talk to me." Riley spoke quietly as he passed Harry Greene.

Noticing the interaction, Nikki watched as the two troopers went into the briefing room and closed the door.

Seeing Jim standing a few feet away, Nikki went over to share what she had seen with him.

"I guess the BCI isn't as close knit as they proclaim to be." Jim ventured to judge.

"Yea, I hope Riley decks him!" Nikki knew that really wouldn't happen. But she couldn't help hoping, since she still had harsh feelings toward Greene from their encounter earlier.

"What's going on between you and Riley? I caught that smile earlier." Jim asked.

A little embarrassed Nikki reminded Jim. "You know I'm really not interested in dating, I'm married to my career!" She giggled.

Nikki however knew down deep she didn't date very often because she had little faith in a relationship with a man. She never really got over being abandoned by her father when she was eight years old. And then having her heart broken when she was a senior in high school didn't help her situation.

They watched as Riley and Greene came back out, neither seemed the worst for wear. "Oh well, maybe next time." Nikki sighed.

Jim laughed to himself, enjoying his partner's sense of humor.

When Mr. and Mrs. Archibald arrived, Frank escorted them to the captain's office as Riley followed. A few minutes later they came out and went into the interrogation room.

After the door to the interrogation room shut, the remaining troopers, Nikki, and Jim went to the adjacent room to see what was about to transpire.

When Nikki was in a position to see through the glass, she saw Sam with his mother next to him with her arm around him, and his father on his other side. Captain Spruce was talking, explaining to

Sam that they only wanted to know where he was Thursday afternoon and evening from about three to nine.

Feeling more comfortable and less threatened with his parents present; Sam cooperated and answered the questions that the captain asked. "I was at work till six, and then I walked home. I got there about six-twenty and ate the dinner my mom had left for me and watched TV. I talked to Penny around eight forty-five for a few minutes and then I went to bed."

"Why did you give the troopers such a hard time son?" His father asked.

"I was scared! I didn't know what they wanted, so I didn't answer the door. I hoped they would just go away."

"Is there something that you're not telling us? My colleagues think your hiding something and they are usually right. If we're not satisfied with your answer you will stay on our radar till this is cleared up." Riley gently explained to Sam.

Sam looked at his mother. "I'm not sure how to tell you?"

His words got everyone's attention. A pin could have dropped in the room where Nikki was and she would have heard it loud and clear. It seemed like an eternity went by instead of the seconds it took Sam to continue his answer.

"I am expecting a baby with Penny. We didn't plan it and were taking precautions. Now we don't know what to do? We were supposed to go to college and now we are going to be parents. I'm sorry. I'm just confused and scared right now for the three of us."

"And Suzy didn't confront you about this at any time?" Asked Riley.

"No, I never talked to her about that."

"Can we go home now Larry?" Maggie Archibald asked. Having known the captain since high school, she was never really comfortable referring to him as Captain Spruce.

"Sure Maggie, I don't see any reason why not, do you Trooper Riley?"

"No, take your son home. I think we're finished here." Riley was disgusted with the situation, trying not to reveal this to the Archibalds as he left.

In the adjacent room, Nikki was not surprised by Sam's answer. She had remembered the interview with Suzy's family on Friday, and what Sam had told her and Jim that Mr. Lamoy had said to him. She believed there was a connection to that and Sam's actions from the start. She also noticed the expression on Riley's face, he was not happy with the way the investigation was going.

Riley left the interrogation room first. Nikki was a little surprised when he walked in the door of the adjacent room where she was. He was noticeably agitated and was not discreet this time when addressing his team.

"We are not here to just end this case by picking someone to be responsible for it! We have to take this more serious and find the killer. Do you understand that?" Riley was trying hard to control himself and keep his voice low so as not to be heard outside the room.

Nikki watched the interaction as the other troopers agreed, realizing this was not the time to voice anything that would push Riley's anger to the next level. She looked over at Greene who was the most vocal. He was standing with his arms folded in silent defiance to Riley's authority more than to what he was saying.

Wayne Kemph spoke up. "He's right and we all know it! This is not a small town crime of passion, that scenario ended when Caesar found victim number two."

Taking a deep breath Riley was a little calmer; Kemph had his back. "Let's all get some rest. The State Police's Violent Crime Investigation Team (VCIT) will be here tomorrow."

CHAPTER FIVE

Investigator Jessica Lewis gathered her belongings and prepared for the hour and forty minute drive from Albany to the Adirondacks. Jessica joined the State Police's Violent Crime Investigation Team three years after becoming a state trooper. She also has access to the New York State Violent Crime Analysis Program (NYS VICAP). The program links patterns of crimes to the FBI's database giving a bigger picture that has helped to solve many crimes across the country that would otherwise take much longer to solve, if they were solved at all.

The drive down the thruway along the Erie Canal and Mohawk River to exit 27 was scenic. Jessica enjoyed looking out the window and taking the time to relax. The mountains and hills seemed to minister to her soul. She had grown up in the country and missed the smells and beauty.

"We get off at the next exit to take Route 30 North." Hearing Mike's voice over the phone, as he talked to the van following them, roused her from daydreaming.

Jessica’s phone rang a moment later. “Hello.” Listening Jessica answered, “You’re not serious, another one.” Mike glanced over at her as she listened intently. “Are you sure that’s the last one there?” … “Okay, we’ll be there in about fifty minutes, talk to you later.” Jessica turned to Mike who had pieced together most of what was going on already.

“There’s a third body, what else?” Mike inquired.

“It’s the oldest. There are just a few bones left, but it’s definitely female. That’s all I know so far, except that they don’t think there are any other remains.”

“Let’s hope not, there is already three too many.” Mike proclaimed with a hint of disgust in his voice.

They rode in silence the rest of the trip as they thought about the murders of three women.

“GPS has us there in five minutes Jess.” Mike announced as he glanced in the rearview mirror to make sure the second vehicle was still behind them.

As they pulled up in front of the station Jessica looked up at the sign. It was weather worn and in need of a paint job, she could easily read the words Mackinaw Village Police Station. "It's ironic, don't you think Mike, we took the Native American's land but named our towns using their language."

"I have wondered about that, actually, especially since we have no idea what the words mean."

"I agree." Jessica replied.

The van pulled up in the space next to them. Roger and Jason got out and began to look around. "Where did they say we were to set up shop?" Jason asked.

Roger pointed down the street. "There's a motel down the road, we have a section on the first floor with the BCI."

The four members of the VCIT entered the station. "Welcome, I'm Officer Frank Bronk. Let me show you to the back where everyone's waiting."

As the four entered the briefing room it became quite crowded. "Hello, I'm glad you're here." Riley walked over and shook the hands of each VCIT member and then introduced them to Captain Spruce, Nikki, and Jim.

After the introduction Riley turned the floor over to Jessica. "Hi everyone, we seem to be a little short on space here, why don't we head over to the motel and set up there. I'm anxious to get going on this, and I'm sure you feel the same. If there is anything you want to bring feel free. We will be spending a great deal of time at the motel and with one another until this is over. Are there any questions?" Jessica waited a few seconds to see if anyone spoke up. "Alright then, let's regroup at the Village Inn."

Nikki went to her desk and watched as the others dispersed and made their way out of the station. Jim was busy collecting the information he had, as was Captain Spruce.

"Nikki why aren't you getting ready to head over to the motel?" Jim wondered seeing her sitting at her desk.

"It will only take me a minute. I'll be ready when you are."

Riley and Jessica walked out of the briefing room. Nikki watched their interaction with curiosity. It was clear Jessica was taking over control of the operation; even Greene seemed to have respect for her.

Nikki opened her top drawer and took out a manila folder and placed it on top of her laptop. She then reached down and unplugged the cord, wound it up and secured it so it wouldn't come unwound. "Ready!"

The motel that they were headed to was the only one in town. It was horse shoe shaped with two floors. This time of year there weren't many rooms that were occupied. Most of its business came in the winter, when snowmobilers came to enjoy the trails that surrounded the area. There wasn't another place for travelers to stay until Middletown which was twenty miles west of Mackinaw. Middletown was a larger village and had a number of hotels and motels.

There was a bustle of activity in the motel lobby and the adjacent hallway containing the seven rooms set aside for the investigation.

There were two adjoining rooms to be used as the briefing area. The motel staff had been instructed earlier in the day from Albany how they wanted the rooms set up. Sleeping arrangements had the four troopers split up, two of them to a room (Harry Greene and Gordon Bleaker returned to Albany after the VCIT arrived). The VCIT had three rooms, one room housed Roger and Jason while Jessica and Mike each had their own rooms.

The motel staff had removed the beds from the two adjoining rooms. One was practically empty with only folding tables and chairs waiting to be arranged. Within an hour the BCI and VCIT had their fax/copy machines, computers, phones, and dry erase boards set up in one of the rooms. The other was set up with two sofas, chairs, folding tables, and a large refrigerator, that the motel brought over from the kitchen. It was filled with different types of beverages and snacks. Two coffee makers were set up and were already brewing fresh coffee as Nikki entered the room to have a look around.

“What do you think? Is there enough room for all of us?” Nikki turned to see Jessica standing behind her.

"Yes, it has all the comforts of home." Nikki joked trying to hide her discomfort with how the investigation was escalating before her eyes.

"Riley tells me you have had some pretty accurate insights on the investigation and that you're not afraid to speak your mind."

"Just doing my job." Feeling like the focus was on her made Nikki even more uncomfortable. Without thought she changed the subject. "How long do you think it will be before we hear from the forensic team?"

The diversion did not go unnoticed by Jessica. "Soon, we are going to have a briefing with what we know so far. There are new developments that you may not have heard yet."

"I'll be waiting."

"Good, I have to go and get ready; the briefing should be in about ten minutes."

Jim finished bringing in the captain's files and then walked over to check in with Nikki. "Look at all this! What a set up!" Jim was impressed with the technology brought in from Albany.

"All these electronics are a little intimidating. I hope we get some answers out of all this?" Nikki remarked.

"I'm sure we will. Did you hear they found remains of a third body?"

Nikki felt chills run up and down her spine. "What did you say?"

"When I was carrying in the box of the captain's files, I heard one of the VCIT guys talking to Kemph. He told him they got a call from Albany before they got here saying that the forensic team found partial remains of another woman this morning."

Frozen in place Nikki suddenly knew they had found Stacey.

"Look at your arms Nikki, are you cold, you have goose bumps!"

"No, it's just the news of the third body. I can't believe this has been going on in our town Jim. Who on earth could be doing this, and for this long without us knowing!" Nikki hesitated before continuing. "Jim, I think it's Stacey."

"What?"

"I think the third body is Stacey."

"Alright, kiddo, take it easy don't get upset over this until we get all the facts. Promise me."

"I'm holding myself together, don't worry."

Jim had worked beside Nikki long enough to know that many times she would have insights into the cases they investigated. But this was a real leap compared to what she usually came up with. Then again this was a bigger case than they had ever encountered. He didn't want to doubt his partner, but at the same time he feared that her being haunted by Stacey's disappearance might have something to do with this. He wondered if it was hopeful thinking on her part more than it was intuition.

"After the briefing lets finish looking at the hospital parking lot tapes, Suzy's purse and keys had to get there somehow." Nikki wanted to keep her focus on the evidence in front of them and off of Stacey.

"Good idea, let's go get a seat and wait for the briefing." Jim was relieved Nikki had changed the subject.

Riley called the briefing together. "Can everyone come into this room and have a seat, we're going to get started." He took a seat in front of Nikki and Jim as Mike Seagal came to the front of the room.

Jessica had a call from Albany and was unable to start the briefing so Mike stepped in. He began by explaining how the Violent Crime Analysis Program (NYS VICAP) would give them an advantage by linking other crimes in New York and the country with similar evidence. That by linking the evidence from different crime scenes it allows them to use it to find the perpetrator. He gave a few examples of cases that were solved by the evidence from one crime shedding light to a similar case that was perpetrated by the same person.

Jessica returned to the room as Mike was finishing.

"Thank you Mike. As some of you may know we have a total of three bodies, all female, placed in the clearing at different times. We know that the latest victim, Suzy Lamoy was stabbed three times. The murder weapon has not been located. The hard fact is that we have a serial killer on our hands. If this person is from here, he does not kill very often which means it may be years before he strikes again. Or there may be other victims if the suspect travels, which could explain the amount of time between the murders. These killers usually commit murders in familiar territory. So who ever this is, he is familiar with this town. Secondly, if he travels and spends time in other areas where he is comfortable, we may be looking for victims there also. The majority of serial killers are not reclusive, social misfits who live alone. They are not outwardly seen as monsters and may not appear strange. Many hide in plain sight within their communities. Serial murderers often have families and homes, are employed, and appear to be normal members of the community. This is why they are often overlooked by law enforcement and the people who know them."

"What we need to do is gather the evidence and see if there is a pattern that matches another case even slightly, and go where the evidence leads. Tomorrow Mike will give a lecture on what a serial killer is and is not, this can shed some light on the personality of the person we are looking for. Are there any questions or comments?" With no one responding, Jessica walked over to the captain. "Captain Spruce I would like to speak with the woman who reported seeing the suspect while hiking as soon as possible."

"I'll have her come to the motel as soon as she can." The captain nodded at Mitch Doogan, a rookie who mainly monitors the traffic in town, and directed him to contact Jill Mayfield and have her come to the motel.

Nikki and Jim went over to an empty desk and hooked up their computers to view the rest of the video from the hospital parking lot. At the 8:45 PM time stamp most of the vehicles that once occupied the parking lot where long gone. The night shift employees parked in a lot on the other side of the hospital leaving the lot with Suzy's car almost empty. "Look Nikki do you see that?" Asked Jim pointing to the lower left corner of the video where a figure in dark clothes and a hood was walking toward Suzy's car. The figure opened the door, threw in what could only be Suzy's purse and then shut the door. The keys must have fallen out before the purse was put into the car. The figure saw them and instead of picking them up he kicked them under the car and slowly walked away with his head down.

"Oh my gosh! That's him isn't it!" Nikki exclaimed. "We need to get this enhanced to see if we can get a better look!"

She went directly to Jessica to tell her their discovery. The group gathered around Nikki's computer to watch the video. Amazed at what they were looking at and the implications, Mike took the video to have it enhanced.

Jessica pulled Nikki aside. "What do you think about that, why would he bother to go to her car and put her purse in it?"

"I think it's odd. He must have wanted us to believe she was abducted from the car, which we did at first." Thinking about what she said Nikki continued. "On the other hand he must know that there are cameras in the parking lot, so why risk it? Why do you think he did it?" Nikki asked Jessica.

"I think he did it to get a thrill out of the risk. He may also believe he won't be caught and thinks he's smarter than us. He covered his identity with his clothing and the time of day he chose. More importantly it may be part of his pattern, a way to find and catch him." Jessica explained. "Oh, and he probably did want us to think he took her from the car. Giving false clues might mean he stuck around to watch us follow them. Another way to get a thrill."

"How did you ever learn so much about this?" Nikki wondered out loud.

"Years of chasing after people like our suspect, reading papers written by profilers who spent their lives also chasing after them. Seems a little morbid doesn't it?" Jessica replied slightly laughing to keep from seeming too serious. The movement at the door caught her attention. "Is that Jill Mayfield over there talking to Mitch?" Jessica asked Nikki.

"Yea it is!"

"Come with me to speak with her." Jessica invited Nikki. They walked toward Jill who now was seated by the window where Mitch had directed her to wait.

"Hello Jill, my name is Jessica Lewis. I'm from the State Police Violent Crime Unit. Do you know Nikki Ardent?"

"Yes, I know Nikki. Why did you want to see me?" Jill was a little nervous and it showed in her voice.

"I understand you had reported what you believed to be a squatter while hiking last Thursday to Les Snell." Jessica stated.

"Yes, that's right."

"I was hoping you might be able to give us more information, more details of the man."

"Well, he was pretty far away, but I suspected he was fairly young. He was pretty agile walking around over there, the ground has fallen trees and rocks everywhere and he had no problems maneuvering with whatever he was carrying. He had to duck to enter under the tree limbs where he went and put down what he had, not a lot though, he bent over enough to not hit his head. He had dark clothes on, pants and long sleeves, no hat though. His hair was dark and on the short side."

"That's excellent Jill. Do you remember anything else, like a specific way he moved his arms, rubbed his head, anything." Jessica asked.

"No, nothing like that. After coming out from the trees he just walked in a straight line the way he had come, nothing unusual about it, sorry."

"Don't be sorry, that's helpful too. You have been very informative, who was hiking with you? Les couldn't recall who you had told him you were with."

"I was with Mary Gurther. She lives over on Elm Street, Nikki knows her. Can I ask why you are looking for this person? Does it have anything to do with the Lamoy's daughter being missing?"

"I can't give you any details, but we are looking into a connection." Jessica believed that people should be aware of what is going on. She didn't want them to feel alienated from the investigation and also felt it helped to keep them safe. "As soon as we speak with the Lamoys we will inform everyone what is happening. In the meantime if you see or remember anything please let us know."

"I will." Jill was a little shocked as she left the makeshift motel room. Not accustomed to having any kind of violent crimes happening where she lived. She now began to face the reality that not only did something happen, but that she was a witness to it. Once in her car, Jill called her best friend Mary to tell her what had happened.

"Do you think the sleeping bag had Suzy Lamoy in it?" Were the first words out of Mary's mouth?

"I don't know but if the state police are investigating it must be something big. They have never been anywhere near this town that I can remember." Jill answered. "They'll probably want to talk to you too; they asked me who I was with."

"That's okay Jill. I don't know what else I can tell them to add to what you have said." Mary knew that she hadn't paid that much attention at the time.

"I'll talk to you later Mary, I don't want to drive away talking on my cell phone."

Laughing slightly Mary answered. "I'll see you later, bye."

After hanging up from speaking with Jill, Mary's phone rang

"Hello."

"Is this Mary Gurther?" Jessica asked.

"Yes it is."

"This is Jessica Lewis from the state police. We're here investigating the disappearance of a local woman and believe you may be able to help us. Can you come over to the motel today?"

"I can come over now." Mary replied hoping to find out more of what was going on.

About a half hour later Mary Gurther arrived at the motel to speak with Jessica.

“I’m glad you were able to come over so soon. Have a seat at my desk Mary.” Jessica motioned toward her desk as she and Mary walked over.

“Nikki, can you join us?” Jessica asked as they walked passed Nikki who was at her desk talking to Jim, and hadn’t noticed Mary’s arrival.

“Mary, we spoke to Jill earlier today. She mentioned that you were with her when you both saw a man in the clearing below the trail you were on Thursday.”

“Yes, that’s right. We had just finished eating and were about to head back down the trail when Jill noticed someone.”

“Can you tell me about the person?”

“I didn’t pay as much attention as Jill did. I only saw him when he walked out from the cluster of trees until he disappeared into the forest. He was dressed in black I think, or very dark blue. He was white, had dark hair that was cut in a regular style man’s cut. The kind that if you go to the barber and just ask for a cut above the ears. That was the only thing I really noticed because I used to be a hair dresser before I got married."

"When he entered into the forest how high on the tree branch was he?"

"Oh my, I don't know. He walked between the trees and then he pushed a branch out of the way, but I wasn't paying enough attention to know which one."

"Thank you, Mary, let me know if you remember anything else."

"Has that young girl been found, was she in the clearing?" Mary inquired.

"I really can't give you any details Mary. But what you and Jill saw has been key to this investigation so far."

"Really! I'm glad we can help." As Mary left she had a strong suspicion that the poor young girl must have been harmed or worse. She called Jill to tell her of her conversation. As they were talking the Lamoys arrived and headed into the motel. Seeing them Mary felt sad. She had a daughter who now lived in

Pennsylvania, and couldn't imagine what it would be like if she were missing. She feared for the news that the Lamoys maybe going to hear.

Riley met the Lamoys in the lobby of the motel and took them to the adjoining motel room. They used the entrance from the hallway instead of going through the room that was occupied with the other members of their team. "I'm sorry but it will be a few minutes. You can take a seat while you wait and help yourself to a drink in the refrigerator."

"We're fine, thank you though." Mr. Lamoy answered for himself and his wife.

Riley excused himself, and went to inform Jessica that the Lamoys had arrived. Jessica was speaking with Nikki and Jim when she looked up and saw Riley heading toward her. "Are they here?"

Riley nodded.

Jessica finished what she was saying before heading toward the other room with Riley. Riley opened the door then closed it behind them as they went to sit by the Lamoys on the sofa.

“Mr. and Mrs. Lamoy, my name is Jessica Lewis, as you may have heard the state police have been brought in to help find your daughter.”

“Yes, we did hear that you were in town.” Marshal Lamoy answered.

“I wish I could be here with some good news, but I’m afraid that isn’t going to be the case.” Reaching over and putting her hand on the top of Joanne Lamoys hand she continued. “The conservation police found the remains of three women Monday morning, I’m afraid Suzy was one of them.”

Joanne Lamoy began to cry as her husband put his arms around her and pulled her toward him. He too was noticeably upset but tried to be strong for his wife.

After a few minutes Marshal looked up and asked. “Where is she now?”

“At the moment she is in Albany, but we will bring her wherever you would like for her burial. When you have contacted a funeral director just let us know.” Moments like this were the worst part of her job. Jessica could never get used to having to tell someone that their loved one was gone, and never returning to them.

Riley explained what he could to the Lamoys about their daughter's final moments, sparing them as much pain as possible. He then offered to have them driven home but Marshal felt he would be able to drive the mile or so they had to go.

When Riley and Jessica finished speaking with the Lamoys, they called everyone together. "It's been a long day, let's get a good night's sleep and meet back here at 9 AM." Jessica was emotionally exhausted after speaking with the Lamoys about the fate of their daughter, and needed to rest before she could do anymore with the investigation. She gathered her belongings and walked down the hall to her room. Once inside she turned on the television and lay on the bed hoping the comedy that was on would distract her for awhile.

Nikki lived a few minutes away by foot. She walked home to her apartment on the second floor of a three story home that was transformed into three separate apartments. It was small, a living room, kitchen, bath, two bedrooms and an outside porch off the kitchen. Just big enough for a chair and small table. "Cindy, Cindy come here, pst pst pst." Nikki called to her cat. She had found her as a small kitten under a porch in town where a stray cat had decided to have her kittens. She was orange with white on her feet, neck and belly.

"There you are silly." Nikki picked her up as she came out from under the kitchen table to rub around Nikki's legs. "I missed you today, let's go relax before dinner." As she lay on her sofa petting Cindy and thinking about the events of the day, her eyes felt heavy. She decided that she better get up and make herself dinner before she fell asleep without anything to eat.

CHAPTER SIX

"What the Hell, how could this have happened?" He blurted out as he sat watching the morning news. Standing up now in his living room, he composed himself and watched the report closely, he didn't want to miss any of the details.

"What's going on? Why are you yelling?" She asked coming into the room drying her hands on a kitchen towel.

"A woman was found murdered up in New York where we use to go on vacation when I was a kid." He answered.

"Oh yea, you mean where you were last week, don't you!" She replied sarcastically as she walked over to him.

He turned so that they were facing one another. Looking into her eyes with a stern expression on his face, he demanded that she come over to him. "Come here." She took a few steps forward. When she was within reach he grabbed her pulling her to him. They kissed passionately, ending only as they both began to giggle. She buried her head into his chest as they hugged; she was glad that he was home with her.

"You know me too well my love!"

"New York is off limits now, right?" She wanted to assure herself.

"Yes, I'm afraid so."

"It will all work out, it always does." She assured him. They kissed quickly, more like a peck, before she headed back to the kitchen to finish cooking breakfast. He went to his computer to look up whatever he could find concerning the news report. There wasn't very much, only that the missing girl's body was found. As he sat back in his chair he wondered if that was the whole truth or if it was all the authorities wanted released. Either way it wasn't good news for him. It was a good thing his business there was done. He would be heading to Virginia for a new project a week from Monday.

~ ~ ~ ~ ~ ~ ~ ~ ~ ~

Nikki pushed her snooze alarm, stretched out on her bed and rolled over on her side. Cindy was lying on the pillow above her head, she reached up to stroke her. "Good morning baby, are you hungry?" Nikki stayed in bed until her alarm went off again.

After turning it off this time, she rolled out of bed and picked up Cindy to carry her to the kitchen to give her breakfast. Nikki gave Cindy a small can of cat food every morning, a ritual Cindy looked forward to and expected. "Looks like salmon dinner for breakfast today sweetie." For herself Nikki made a bowl of oatmeal with raisins and brown sugar, she then went to take her shower and get ready for work.

When she arrived at the motel the troopers were already moving about taking reports off the fax and looking at their computer screens.

"Good morning Nikki, we've had some developments. VICAP started printing out information shortly after we put in the details of the case. It seems there was another woman found in 2004 in Pennsylvania that might have been attacked by the same person who attacked Suzy. The reason that we believe it may have been the same person is the way she was stabbed. Whoever it was used the same type of knife, possibly the exact same knife. It is a type of kitchen knife for slicing meat, which can be purchased just about any place. They were both stabbed three times once in the liver and once in each kidney. The bleeding in these areas is immense, and they would have bled out in a relatively short time." Jessica explained.

"How do you know it was the same knife?" Nikki wondered.

"The forensic team is able to measure the wound for size and shape of the weapon. The measurements are the exact same in both cases. Mike has the details and will be giving a briefing when everyone is here."

"Jessica, if this woman was killed in Pennsylvania and it was the same person who did it, then he can't live around here. That means we can start with vacationers who live in Pennsylvania and visit here on a regular basis." Excited that they now had a direction to start their search, Nikki couldn't wait to get started.

When she saw Jim come into the room Nikki went over to fill him in on what Jessica had told her. They then walked over to the adjoining room to join the troopers and get a fresh cup of coffee while waiting for the briefing. When they walked in Troopers West and Hines where cracking jokes and telling stories of funny moments that occurred in cases they had been involved in. Jim also had a few stories and he joined in on the conversation.

Nikki was leaning up against the counter sipping at her cup of coffee, enjoying the tales she was hearing. She couldn't help but laugh. It was nice to feel a light heart after the developments of this past week.

Poking his head into the doorway Investigator Roger Leary interrupted the camaraderie. "Hey guys, Mike is ready to do the briefing."

The group filtered into the briefing area and took their seats. Mike Seagal was leafing through papers putting them in the order he wanted before walking over to the front of the room.

"Good morning everyone. It's time to really get into the nitti gritty of this investigation. We have received all of the forensic team's results so far and the information from NYS VICAP. First of all let's remember to separate fact from fiction when it comes to dealing with this unknown perpetrator. Forget everything you have heard from different forms of the media concerning serial killers. Most of that information is fictional or half true at best. There is no common pattern that creates a serial killer. Their personal reasons to pursue their crimes are the most important factor to our investigation. They are each driven by their own unique motives or reasons. An inclination to become a serial killer, much like other violent offenses, is biological, social, and psychological in nature, and it is not limited to any specific characteristic or trait. The development of a serial killer involves a combination of these factors, which exist together in a rare union in certain individuals. They have the right biological predisposition, shaped by their psychological nature.

Serial killers are not limited to any specific group, such as being male, any certain age, race, or religion. The fallacy that white males are the usual serial killers is just that, a fallacy. There have been serial killers in all cultures and races. They tend to be the same race, religion and culture as the areas they live in. Since this is a predominantly white community, our killer is most likely white and male.

They use a mixture of charm, manipulation, intimidation, and occasionally violence to control others, in order to satisfy their own selfish needs. Their personality traits include glibness, superficial charm, having a sense of self-worth, pathological lying, and the manipulation of others.

Their emotional traits include a lack of remorse and/or guilt, shallowness, a lack of empathy, and failure to accept responsibility. Their lifestyle behaviors include stimulation-seeking behavior, impulsivity, irresponsibility, and a lack of realistic life goals. Their anti-social behaviors include poor behavioral controls, early childhood behavior problems, and juvenile delinquency. The combination of these traits, styles, and socially abnormal lifestyles can manifest themselves differently in individual psychopaths. Psychopaths who commit serial murder do not value human life and are extremely callous in their dealings with their victims. For the most part, serial murder involves strangers with no visible relationship between the offender and the victim.

Motive generally may be difficult to determine in a serial murder investigation. But regardless of the motive, serial murderers commit their crimes because they want to. Motives in other killers have been anger, in which an offender displays rage or hostility. Power or thrill has been seen as a motivation in which the offender feels empowered and/or excited when he kills his victims. Sex has also been seen as a motivation when the perp is driven by sexual needs and desires. There may or may not be sexual contact during the murder. The killer selects their victim based upon availability, vulnerability, and attraction; no matter what their motive may be."

"Now let's discuss what we have so far. Suzy was taken last Thursday after three in the afternoon. We still do not know exactly where this occurred. The killer returned her purse and keys to her car Thursday evening after placing her body in the Adirondack Park. This was witnessed by Jill Mayfield and Mary Gurther early Thursday evening around five o'clock. She was stabbed three times prior to being placed at the scene."

"After putting the information we had into the NYS VICAP system we found out that there was another victim in 2004 in

Pennsylvania near Wilkes-Barre. Her name was Nancy Walnick she was found ten days after she went missing with the same wounds as Suzy Lamoy. We know that there was no sexual contact between the perpetrator and Suzy, neither was there any with the 2004 victim in Pennsylvania. The second body found here has been identified as Melanie Short, a 22 year old from New York City who went missing in 2010. She was last known to be headed to the Albany/Troy area on a bus. She had three knife wounds similar to the other two victims. The third body has not been identified yet. DNA has been sent for processing, the skull has not been found so we cannot use dental records to identify her. But there were similar knife marks on two ribs that would indicate stab wounds by the liver and at least one of her kidneys. We believe she was killed eight to ten years ago."

Hearing the time frame of eight to ten years Nikki felt a little nauseous. She looked at Jim who was already looking at her; they both knew what they were thinking.

Mike was continuing. "As far as the forensic evidence goes we are still waiting for the final results on fibers, fingerprints, and biological evidence. There were none of these at the site in Pennsylvania, hopefully there will be here. Does anyone have any questions or comments?"

With no one having questions, Jessica thanked Mike and took over the meeting from there. "We are going to break up into groups. Nikki and Jim, could you two continue to follow up at the hospital and see if you can figure out how Suzy was abducted from there. Find out who was working that day and start there, also any other footage from videos within the hallways or at other exits could help. Riley and Kemph can you contact Wilkes-Barre and see if there is anything that is not mentioned within the reports we have here. Also see if anything has come up since, and see if a trip there may be beneficial for us. Troopers Hines and West check in town and in Middletown for a list of names of travelers around that time. Check hotels, motels, bed and breakfasts, anyplace that would have lodged someone. Leary and Deacon can you go over to the Conservation Police Barracks and see if there is any record or way to find out who was in that area last Friday. The unknown perp must have driven there, see where he could have parked a vehicle to enter into the area we found the women. Maybe there will be tire tracks. Mike and I will stay here and continue to work on the NYS VICAP information. Report in as you find anything no matter how small it may seem, even insignificant."

When Nikki and Jim arrived at the hospital they went to the security office first to see if there were any other tapes they could look at. There were video cameras for all the parking areas but they didn't have any in the hospital except by the pharmacy. The Chief of Security said he would collect the footage from Thursday afternoon and evening. They could take it with them when they headed back to the station. Their next step was the personnel office to get the names of all the employees who worked that day. The VP of Human Resources was happy to assist and began to gather the information for them.

"Hello officers." Nikki and Jim turned to see who was speaking to them. "I'm John Sage the CEO of the hospital; my staff will assist you in any way possible. I have set aside a room we usually use for meetings, if you would like to conduct your interviews with the staff there. It may be more comfortable."

“Thank you.” Nikki replied. “That would be a big help for us and give some privacy to the staff.”

“Alright then, if you will follow me I’ll take you to the meeting room. Mrs. Albright will you see who is working today, and who is available to meet with the officers please.”

“Right away, I’ll start bringing them down in a few minutes.”

Nikki and Jim followed John Sage down the hall and around a corner to the meeting room. As they entered the room Nikki noticed how nice it was, the chairs were a lighter shade of brown leather, with significant padding. There was a large table in the center of the room with the chairs surrounding it. A projector hung from the ceiling, and there was a screen for the projector that was rolled up above a blackboard.

“This is a very nice room. I think it will do very well. Thank you.” Nikki said as she looked around the room.

“It’s our pleasure, being such a small hospital we all know each other in some capacity. Suzy was very well liked and respected here.” John Sage was slightly emotional as he spoke about Suzy.

"I have a daughter her age. She's in college out of state right now. I can't even imagine the pain her parents must be feeling."

The staff from the kitchen entered the room with bottles of water on ice, coffee, tea and the necessary condiments to go with them. "Thank you, Mark. You can set them up on the side there." John Sage pointed to another table to the right of the door. "If there is anything else you need my extension is 7835. There's a phone on the wall next to the door. I expect the staff will be coming in shortly."

"Thank you. You didn't have to go to all this trouble, but we appreciate it." Jim said shaking hands with John Sage as he left the room.

Nikki and Jim helped themselves to refreshments. Nikki took a bottle of water, and Jim a cup of coffee. They settled down at the far end of the table preparing to interview the staff. A few minutes later there was a knock on the door and Mrs. Albright entered with the first of the staff who had worked last Thursday.

They were two hours into their interviews with no leads at all when a young man came in. Mrs. Albright introduced him as Jack Sandler one of the Environmental Services Technicians.

“Hello Jack, my name is Jim and this is Nikki. We understand you were working last Thursday, and were here between two forty-five and five o’clock.”

“Yes sir, I was. I was mopping the floors on the first floor, the section called one north.”

“Did you know Suzy Lamoy?” Nikki asked.

“I knew what she looked like. She would say goodnight to me as she left the building. She would say hello and goodbye to everyone.”

“Did you see her last Thursday that you remember?” Nikki asked.

“I passed her in the hall. She didn’t say anything though, she looked a little upset. And she seemed to be in a hurry.”

“Was she heading out the way she usually would go?” Nikki asked hoping he would have paid attention.

"Yes, she did. I remember watching her because it bothered me that she appeared upset. I thought that she spoke with someone down the end of the hall. She hesitated at the turn toward the hall where the door is. And I thought I saw an arm reach out to her, like someone was putting their arm around her shoulders. But then she was out of site. I didn't go down to look. I wish I had now."

"Can you take us to the spot where this occurred, son?" Jim asked but already knew the answer.

"Of course, it's not far from here."

Nikki, Jim and Jack walked down the hall to the other side of the hospital. Jack showed them about where he was, the route Suzy took, and the spot where she had turned the corner to leave the hospital. After turning the corner she would have gone about ten feet to the door. Nikki looked up and down the corridor for cameras but there weren't any. She went out the door and noticed a camera at the far corner of the building. "Is that the camera that took the parking lot video we saw already, Jim?" She asked pointing toward it.

“I’m not sure, we’ll have to ask security.” Jim called the security office with his cell and the guard on duty came down to meet them.

They walked toward the lot and showed the security guard where Suzy’s car had been. Then pointed to the camera to see if that would have been the camera that took the footage they watched earlier in the week.

“No, that camera went out of commission on Tuesday a week ago. We have to get the company to come and replace it. The camera that we had the footage from was from the corner of the building over there to the left. The two cameras cover basically the same area. The one that’s not working picked up more of the area to the right that was a blind spot. The two cameras on the ends of the building couldn’t pick up directly in front of the walkway. There’s a ten foot blind spot so we installed the camera in the middle for that reason.”

“Do you know what is wrong with the camera, why it stopped working?” Nikki asked.

“We think water got into it somehow and short circuited the wiring.”

“Can we have the name of the company that will be exchanging the camera?” Jim asked.

“Of course, I’ll get it for you and bring it to the conference room.” The security guard replied as he walked toward the door, he had gotten a call and needed to respond to a situation.

“That is awful convenient isn’t it?” Nikki remarked, not expecting an answer from Jim or Jake.

“Jake can you tell me how many employees leave using this door?” Jim was wondering how secluded the exit was.

“A few, most park in the front lot. This is the overflow parking area.”

“Do you recall anyone who may have left shortly before or after Suzy did?” Jim asked.

“There wasn’t anyone that I recall on that day. The next person that I remember leaving was June. She’s a nurse on the first floor.

I don't know her last name but she left as I was finishing up, about fifteen minutes later."

"Is there anything else you can think of that would be helpful that you might have noticed?" Jim inquired.

"I don't think so, but if I think of anything I could call the station. Would that be okay?"

"Sure son, let me write the number down for you. We are conducting the investigation out of the motel with the state troopers so the number is different. But if you lose this number you can always call the station." Jim handed Jake the number to the motel room before he walked away to return to work.

"So, Suzy spoke to her sister when she was in the locker room and left there. By the time she got to the first floor she was upset and possibly met up with someone. Do you think she spoke with someone else over the phone in between?" Nikki questioned.

"I don't know but I think we need to narrow down the phone call she got from her sister to be sure of the timing. I'll report in with what we've found here and ask about Suzy's phone records, maybe they came in." Jim remarked.

They headed back to the conference room where Mrs. Albright was waiting with another employee. Nikki took her into the room while Jim asked if Mrs. Albright could find Cindy so that they could speak with her again.

He then phoned into the makeshift motel headquarters to speak with Jessica. He explained to her what they had found out at the hospital so far, including the need to watch the rest of the parking lot video from the camera they had not had a chance to view yet. Jessica agreed that the phone records where important and said she would try to put a rush on them.

When Jim returned to the conference room Nikki was finishing up with the young woman and Mrs. Albright had arrived with Cindy.

"Hello Cindy, we had you come to see us today because we wanted to review the phone call of Suzy's that you overheard. You said that she received the call while in the locker room and said she would meet them in a half hour. Did she seem upset after that?" Nikki asked.

"No, not at all, she acted like she hadn't spoken to anyone. She kept talking with us as we left for home."

"How far did you walk with her?"

"Kadi and I parked in the front lot and went down the hall to the left when we left the locker room. Suzy went to the right toward the back lot."

"Did her phone ring, or did you see her answer her phone a second time?"

"No. Kadi and I were talking."

"Okay Cindy, sorry to bring you here again we thought there may have been a second phone call. You can go back to work now." Nikki said, frustrated over not getting any further information.

Mrs. Albright brought June to the conference room next. She had left from the same door as Suzy that Thursday.

"Hello June, my name is Nikki. Jim and I are investigating Suzy Lamoy's murder. What time did you leave work last Thursday, and what exit did you use?"

"I know I left out the door to the back lot because I always park there. I would have to ask what time I punched out to be sure, but I believe it was about three-fifteen. I usually leave around that time."

"Did you see Suzy Lamoy or anything unusual?"

"No, I didn't see her, and nothing caught my eye. I wish I could be of more help."

"If you do recall anything as time goes by please give us a call, okay." Nikki was getting tired. They had been interviewing the hospital staff for three and a half hours with no leads other than what Jack Sandler had told them. She wanted to return to the motel and look in another direction.

"I will, is it okay if I go now?" June asked.

"Yes, of course." Nikki said.

As June went out the door Nikki looked at Jim. “I really don’t want to do this anymore today, how about you?”

“I think we’re done. Mrs. Albright doesn’t seem to have anyone else.” Jim said as he noticed Mrs. Albright entering the room alone.

“That’s all the staff that was working that day. Is there anything else I can do for you?”

“I think we’re done for now.” Jim answered. “We can see ourselves out.”

“Okay, hope you catch whoever did this. I for one cannot sleep very well knowing he is out there.” Explained Mrs. Albright.

“We’re doing our best, we want him too.” Jim related to what she was saying, he had a hard time sleeping well himself.

As he and Nikki left the room and headed down the hallway they decided to stop by the security office. They wanted to pick up the name of the company who fixes the video cameras, since the security guard had not brought it to them, as well as the other camera footage.

The security guard was heading into his office when they arrived. "Hey officers, there was trouble with a patient who is detoxing. I couldn't get back to the office till just now, hold on a second." The guard went to a cabinet and took out a file. He made a copy of a piece of paper from the file and handed it to Jim. "That's the company's name, address and phone number, hope it helps." He also handed Jim the copy of the video from the cameras.

"We do too, thank you." Jim replied.

"Let's stop and grab a bite to eat before returning to the motel Jim. I'm starving, all this talking has given me an appetite." Nikki said sarcastically.

"I would love a juicy burger, how about you?"

"The juicier the better." Nikki replied.

CHAPTER SEVEN

"Yes, I understand. I'll ask her when she gets back. I'll meet up with you soon. Yes sir. Have a good day."

Nikki overheard Jessica as they entered the motel room and knew instinctively that it had something to do with her. "Hi Jessica, we're back from the hospital. Jim told you about the conversation we had with Jack Sandler. We think Suzy may have had another phone call after her sister. What do you think?"

"I think that it may very well be a possibility. Jim the phone records just came in. There on my desk, can you start going through them? I need to speak with Nikki in private." Jessica led the way to her motel room down the hall.

Once in the room Jessica shut the door and turned to Nikki. "The FBI is going to take over the case starting tomorrow morning. Because of the body in Pennsylvania having a matching profile the killer has crossed state lines and that puts the case in their hands instead of ours. The Special Agent in charge is going to be Daniel

Dillon, I've worked with him before. He would like it if you and I join him on this case." Jessica explained.

"What, why me? I have no training in these types of investigations. Besides, Jim is my partner. I can't walk out on him!" Shocked at the invitation Nikki spoke before thinking.

"I'm afraid that your reputation for good instincts is something that many in law enforcement have heard about. Daniel, being one of them, would like to give you a chance to move up in your career. That's if you're interested." Jessica continued to explain.

"Can I sleep on it? This comes out of the blue, and I wasn't expecting it."

Jessica laughed, "Of course you can, and you don't have to give me your decision until late tomorrow. Daniel will want to know when he gets here."

Nikki laughed too. "There's no pressure is there?"

"When Daniel recommended me to head up the VCIT, I was shocked. Then he wanted an answer in three hours! He's a great guy with a unique sense of humor. But he's all business when it comes to murderers. He is relentless and won't stop till this guy is found."

"I can't wait to meet him. We seem to have the same feelings about this guy." Nikki's curiosity was peaked now. If Daniel truly would not stop till this guy is found, she might finally find out what happened to Stacey.

There was a knock at the door. "Nikki, Nikki I need to see you!" It was Jim, the DNA results were back on the third body.

Nikki opened the door. "Can I come in with you and Jessica?" Nikki looked at Jessica who nodded her head. "Of course." She opened the door to let Jim in. He was obviously unnerved about something. He sat down in a chair in Jessica's room and took a deep breath. "You were right Nikki, the DNA results are back on the third body. It's Stacey Bernard! They matched the remains to her mother's DNA. There's no doubt about it, it's her!"

"Are you alright Nikki?" Jessica asked. Nikki had sat on Jessica's bed without saying a word and just starred at the floor. "Nikki!"

"Yeah. I'm okay. I knew, but hearing it confirmed, wow. It's been so long since she went missing. I just need a few minutes, I'm sorry." Nikki was feeling a lot of emotion: relief, shock, and anger all at the same time. She wanted to cry at the finalization that she would never see her friend again, and over the knowledge that she had been brutally murdered, but couldn't.

"Will you be alright kiddo? I should get back. Suzy did get another phone call and I'm trying to find out who made it." Jim said reluctantly, not wanting to leave Nikki but felt that this lead was important.

"Yeah, I'll be fine. I'll be there in a minute. Go do what you can to find out who it was."

"Do you want to be alone? You can stay here as long as you need to." Jessica said putting her hand on Nikki's shoulder.

"Thank you, I won't be long. I really want to get the man who did this." Nikki looked up at Jessica, as the two made eye contact Jessica saw the inner strength that Nikki had. She had no doubt that Nikki would get him.

Once Jim and Jessica left the room, Nikki took her wallet out of her pocket. Opening it she took out a picture of Stacey. "I promised I would find you one day. Now I promise you I will catch whoever did this to you. He robbed us of a life of friendship, he stole you from me, and I cannot forgive or forget that." Nikki looked at the picture of her best friend a few more seconds before putting the photo back into her wallet. She took a deep breath and wiped the tear from her cheek before heading out of Jessica's room to join the rest of the team.

She approached Jim. He was sitting at a desk using a computer to try and find the owner of the phone number that was on Suzy's phone. "Any luck with the phone number?"

"Not really. Someone called her five minutes after her sister, the call lasted thirty seconds. The number is from a burner phone that was purchased with cash. It's a dead end." Jim slammed his hand down on the desk attracting the attention of the room. "Sorry, this is just so damn frustrating."

"Let's take a break. I have something to talk to you about." Nikki said to Jim as she put her arm around his walking with elbows locked to the break area. "Do you want a cup of coffee or something?" Nikki inquired.

"No coffee, some ice water would be nice. I feel a little dry." Jim explained.

"Sure thing partner." She handed Jim a glass of ice water. "Jessica told me that the case is going to be handed over to the FBI tomorrow." Nikki revealed to Jim.

"I was wondering when that would happen ever since I heard of the victim in Pennsylvania. But why did she have to tell you that in private?"

"There's more to it than that. Evidently the special agent who is in charge, a Daniel Dillon, has heard of some of the cases we have solved here. He wants me to be on his team when he goes to search for the killer. I don't want to do it without you though."

"Nikki, we have been partners a long time. But we both know that I would not have solved half of the crimes by myself that we have solved together. You're the one with the talent. This would be a wonderful opportunity for you kiddo, don't pass it up. Promise me you won't pass this up because of me!"

Nikki looked at her partner, they were good friends, and he was a surrogate father to her. "I really want to catch this guy and Jessica will be with me, I trust her. She knows Daniel and says he doesn't stop until he finds who he is looking for."

"I think you will fit in just right with the team. Besides I'm married. I don't think my wife and kids would want to travel all over the country, living out of a suitcase till this guy is in custody. Don't forget it's almost summer! Swimming and camping are the only plans they have! James Jr. has a girlfriend now and that would complicate the sleeping arrangements. I would get no sleep at all keeping my eye on the two of them all night!"

Nikki and Jim laughed at the thought of his family going on the search for the killer with them.

“They do have pools at most motels these days, and I’m sure there are plenty of campgrounds you could stay at.” Nikki joked back at him.

After a few seconds Nikki and Jim’s thoughts turned back to the case. “Let’s look at those other tapes from the hospital before we call it a day. Once the FBI gets here we may not get the time.” Jim suggested.

“Yea, that’s a good idea.” Nikki removed the tapes from the case they were in and plugged them into the computer on her desk. They watched the tape from the other side of the parking lot first, from two thirty to four in the afternoon. Suzy was not in the video but there were two cars that left the parking area at the same time she would have been taken. One was a Chevy Cavalier that was dark in color. The video was black and white so it could have been dark blue, black, or any other shade that was dark. The other was a Volkswagen Jetta that was a lighter color. The license plates could not be seen.

"Let's get the hospital security to see if any employees have cars like those. I'll call over to see while you load the next tape. Maybe they saw something?" Jim suggested.

"Sure, sounds like a plan." Nikki replied.

A few minutes later the two were viewing another of the hospital videos from the area outside the pharmacy. They next watched videos from the side parking lot, and finally the front of the hospital but saw nothing of any use.

"It looks like we're the last ones working tonight!" Jim looked up after the final tape had ended and saw an empty room.

"Yes it does. I suppose we should call it a night and start again tomorrow. It's almost six o'clock and I have a pizza with my name on it waiting for me." Nikki had ordered a pizza for pick up from the local pizza pallor. She hadn't had time for grocery shopping and was running out of ingredients at home to make anything.

"I'm sure Laura has dinner ready. She'll start to worry so I better be on my way. I'll see you tomorrow bright and early."

When Nikki arrived the next morning she noticed a van that had not been there previously. “That must be the FBI team’s van.” She thought out loud. She entered the motel and went to the room down the hall and noticed two new faces. There was a man in his late twenties with blonde hair and another in his mid-thirties with black hair. Both were wearing suits and ties.

Jessica looked up and saw that Nikki had just arrived. “Nikki, come on over I want to introduce you to Daniel Dillon and Justin Forest.”

When Nikki approached the two men they shook her hand. “Hello, I’m Justin Forest.” The dark haired man said as he introduced himself.

“And I’m Daniel Dillon.” The younger blonde man said. “I’m really glad to meet you Miss Ardent.”

Nikki couldn’t help but notice how warm his brown eyes felt as she looked into them. “Please, call me Nikki.” She replied surprised that Daniel was the younger of the two. She felt herself blush as she realized she was attracted to the young FBI agent. It made her feel insecure and she didn't like to feel that way. She wasn't very good at relationships, especially in the beginning of one. She had trust issues with men when she found them attractive. She would find herself caught in the middle of being attracted to someone and not wanting to be at the same time.

"Jessica told me that she filled you in on who I want on my team for this one, what do you say Nikki?" Daniel asked.

"I want nothing else but to get this guy, so yes, I want to be on the team!" Nikki wanted to keep things professional and not let them get personal. She had mastered the ability to push her feelings down inside of her so that they wouldn't be noticed by others, or felt by her.

"That's great!" Daniel said with a smile. He usually got what he wanted, and Nikki was who he wanted. "Today and tomorrow, if necessary, we will spend gathering the information together here before moving on." Daniel then turned to the group. "Let's come together and discuss the information we have gathered over the last few days. Jessica and Mike is there anything new from forensics?"

"No, unfortunately, there were no fibers, body fluids, fingerprints or other evidence on the bodies of Suzy Lamoy or Mellany Short. The third body was identified as Stacey Bernard who went missing from this town eight years ago. She and Suzy were locals but Mellany was from New York City. She was last known to be in the Albany-Troy area. How she ended up in this area is unknown." Jessica replied.

Daniel next addressed Riley and Kemph. "Is there anything new to add from Pennsylvania, with the Nancy Walnick case?"

Riley spoke for both of them. "Yes there is, we spoke to the officers from the town of Wilkes-Barre where her body was found. It seems that Nancy received a phone call just before she disappeared. Her roommate was at home with her when she answered the call. The person on the other end told her that her mother had been hurt in a car accident. That she needed to come to the local hospital to sign consent forms for her to be treated. She was upset and left in a hurry after telling her roommate where she was going. The truth was that her mother was not in any accident and no one had called her on an official bases. The killer must have phoned her to get her into the open. He must have chosen her, stalked her, and then attacked her using the phone call to make her vulnerable."

"Thank you Trooper Riley."

"Anything from the motels, Troopers Hines and West?" Daniel inquired.

"We checked with this motel and there were no out of town male guests around the time of Suzy's disappearance. There were just the usual clients. A meeting of the local Women's Christian Group that had a few out of town female members present." Hines reported.

"In Middletown there were two out of town guests at the three motels there. One was a family who is looking to relocate and was staying in town looking at properties. And the other was a business man from Pennsylvania. He was finalizing a purchase for a land company out of Pennsylvania, The Oak Tree Land Development Corporation. He had stayed there a total of three times over the last year. They described him as pleasant, business like, but not very social. He checked out the Monday morning after Suzy was murdered. Unfortunately we did not get a name. The room was rented by the company, via the internet, prior to his arrival each time. We did get a good description of him but the motel doesn't have cameras. He is about five feet eight inches, black hair, and light blue eyes. According to the front desk clerk, he was rather good looking, dressed neat and tipped the cleaning staff and wait staff rather well." West added.

"We called the Oak Tree Land Development Corporation but they wouldn't give us any information without a warrant. They told us that their employees have all had background checks and would not have been hired if they had any criminal background. So far we have not found a judge to give us a warrant without any significant evidence." Hines continued.

Investigators Leary and Deacon were next, motioning to them Daniel continued. "Did you find anything out from the conservation police investigation?"

"We spoke to Lester Snell, David Morgan and Luther Martin. They scoured the forest and the roads leading up to the entrances to the area where the women were found and they didn't find anything. The dirt roads are very rocky and tires don't leave marks on them. There were no legible footprints either. Unfortunately we hit a dead end." Investigator Deacon answered.

"Thank you everyone. As you know this case has now been handed over to the FBI. Jessica Lewis and Nikki Ardent are going to join Justin Forest and myself as we continue the investigation. This doesn't mean that you cannot continue to investigate. If you find any information that is relevant please forward it to us. I will leave my number, as well as the rest of the team's numbers, in case you need to contact us. The Bureau appreciates the time and effort you have put into the investigation and I will keep you posted of any progress we make. I plan on winding things up here and moving on by tomorrow. Are there any questions?"

"Alright then we have a few loose ends to tie up. Nikki and Jim can you continue to follow up with the hospital, see if they can identify the two cars that were leaving the parking lot? Jessica and

Justin can you go to Middletown with a sketch artist and see if the desk clerk, or anyone else, can give us a good description of the business man that was staying there?" Daniel asked.

They all agreed to follow up with the loose ends. Jim called the hospital security office to see if they had found out who the two cars belonged to. They knew that the Chevy Cavalier belonged to one of the care attendants who worked in the ER. She told them that she didn't remember seeing anything unusual when she left work that day. The VW's owner had not been identified as yet. It was not registered to anyone who worked at the hospital, but it may belong to a visitor of a patient in the ICU. According to the security guard on duty, they had asked all the patients if any of their visitors had a car that fit that description. A family member who was visiting in ICU was going to check with the patient's grandmother to see if she was there that day. Her car was a tan VW Jetta. The security guard would call Jim as soon as he knew.

Jessica and Justin headed to Middletown with Judy Swanson, who was a local artist. It was a forty minute drive down a two lane road. Most of the scenery consisted of trees and hay fields. An occasional farm house and barn could be seen with Holstein dairy cows grazing in the fields around them.

They had called ahead so that the desk clerk would be available to speak with them when they arrived. They pulled into the parking lot of the Middletown Eastern Holiday Motel and found a parking spot across from the main entrance. They entered the main lobby and went to the front desk, Jessica approached the clerk. "Hello, we are here from the FBI to speak with the clerk who was on duty last Monday morning. I believe her name is Maryanne Arbor."

"We were expecting you, come with me." The clerk said.

The clerk led them down the hallway to the right of the lobby. When they arrived at a door marked 'office' she knocked. A voice on the other side acknowledged the knock. "Come in." They walked through the door that led to a small office. An older man was sitting behind the desk and a younger woman was sitting in a chair in front of the desk. They stood to greet their guests and introduce themselves. "Hello my name is John Rogers, I'm the day manager. This is Maryanne Arbor the desk clerk that you wanted to speak with."

"Nice to meet you both, is it okay to conduct our business in this office?" Jessica inquired.

"Yes, I can get a few more chairs. Or you can use one of our rooms, which might be better, you would have more room." John Rogers suggested.

"What do you think Judy, would you be more comfortable in a room?" Jessica asked.

"Yes, I'd rather be in a room. I think it would be more relaxing for Maryanne." Judy responded.

"Follow me then. There is a room not far from here you can use." John Rogers led them back down the hall toward the front desk. They turned to the right and down another hall to a room numbered 100. "This room should suffice." John said as he used a key card to open the door. He stood back to allow the rest of them to enter the room. "If there is anything you need, or anything I can get you don't hesitate to ask. There is bottled water in the small refrigerator. There is also a coffee pot with tea bags and coffee packets, feel free to use any of them. I will be around if you need me."

"Thank you, John." Jessica replied as he closed the door and left them alone with Maryanne to conduct their interview.

Jessica and Justin took seats over by the window out of Judy's way as she and Maryanne made themselves comfortable at the small table against the wall. Judy set up her sketch materials while Maryanne sat in the chair opposite her at the table. "Try to relax Maryanne. Close your eyes if you need to, go back to last Monday morning when the man from the Oak Tree Land Development Corporation checked out and describe him to me. Take your time; we're not in a hurry."

Maryanne relaxed, took a few deep breaths and began to describe the man she checked out. "He was average, about five foot eight I think, his hair was neat, cut short above his ears, thick though and black. His eyes were blue, really light blue, and I remember his eye lashes were long."

“You’re doing good Maryanne. What shape was his face?” Judy asked.

“Kind of oval, but not too thin”

“And his nose?” Judy began to lead her into giving details she may otherwise have overlooked.

“Small, his eyes were more noticeable.”

“Very good, Maryanne, tell me about his chin.”

“Nothing really comes to mind to mention about his chin. I remember that he was clean shaven. Oh and his ears were close to his head, not very big.”

“Did he have any scars, moles or other marks that you can remember?”

“No, he was attractive. But too old for me. I think he was over thirty.”

“Take a look at the picture that I’ve drawn based on your description, let me know if anything needs to be changed.” Judy turned the sketch pad so that it faced Maryanne as she opened her eyes.

"Yes, that's almost him. His chin had more of a point to it, and he had side burns. But not too long, down to the middle of his ears."

Judy made changes to the sketch and showed Maryanne the sketch again.

"Yes, yes, that's him!" Maryanne exclaimed.

Jessica and Justin came over to look at the sketch. "Thank you, Maryanne. You have been a big help to us." Jessica said.

"Is he the one you are looking for?" Maryanne asked.

"We don't know, Maryanne, we're just tying up loose ends." Jessica explained.

Judy gathered her materials together and the four walked out to the lobby. John Rogers was behind the desk with the clerk cashing out the registers. "Are you done already?" He asked.

"Yes. Maryanne has a good memory, she was a big help." Jessica said as she patted Maryanne on the back.

"Are you heading back to Mackinaw now? Or can we offer you lunch in the restaurant?" John Rogers asked.

"We need to get back as soon as we can. But thank you for the invitation." Jessica explained.

"How about sandwiches to go?" John didn't want them to leave on empty stomachs.

"That would be great, thank you." Justin piped in. He was getting hungry and knew they had a long drive ahead of them.

John Rogers made a call and less than ten minutes later two waitresses came out with bags of sandwiches, cans of soda, and chips for them to take with them.

"I hope you catch whoever hurt that poor girl in Mackinaw." John said as he walked them to their car. "Let me know if we can be of further assistance."

"We will, thank you very much for the lunch." Jessica said as she shut her car door.

They all waived good bye as they pulled out of the parking lot. "Maryanne was very impressive." Justin remarked as he turned onto the road back to Mackinaw.

"Yes, I think she was attracted to him. That's why she remembered him so clearly. According to this sketch he is a very good looking man." Judy expressed her opinion of the situation. "How could someone so handsome do something so horrible?"

"We're just working the case. He may not have done anything, he might have just been here for business and went back home. But we have to check everything so we don't miss something." Jessica explained.

"That makes sense." Judy agreed.

When they arrived back at the motel in Mackinaw, Judy took her car and went back to her studio while the others went into the motel. The rooms were almost empty, Daniel had dismantled the equipment and had it boxed up. Jim and Nikki were helping him. Everyone else had headed back to their prior jobs in Mackinaw and Albany.

“How did you make out?” Daniel asked.

“Good. Maryanne, the clerk on duty last Monday, gave us an excellent description.” Jessica took the sketch out and passed it to Daniel, who began to pass it around the room.

“Anyone recognize him?” Daniel asked.

“He doesn’t look familiar.” Jim remarked, as he passed the sketch to Nikki.

“I’ve never seen him before either, let’s take the sketch to the hospital and see of anyone there recognizes him.”

“Jim do you mind doing that?” Daniel asked. “I wanted to keep Nikki here to prepare for the next couple days.”

“Sure, no problem. I’ll find out if they identified the owner of the VW while I’m there too.” Jim said as he took the sketch and headed out the door.

CHAPTER EIGHT

The late May morning was warm as he sat outside drinking a cup of coffee, enjoying the smells of spring in the country. It was Saturday morning and he only had a week before he was heading to Virginia. He had some preparations to make before leaving and didn't want to wait till the last minute.

"Hey Hun?" He called.

"Coming." She said as she came out and sat on the porch in the chair that was next to him. "What a beautiful morning, don't you think?"

"I thought so too, the spring has always been my favorite season. It feels like a time when everything can be renewed, changed, started over." He continued. "I got the cell phones out of the basement, when I leave check yours morning, noon, and night. I'll do the same. If one of us sends the code word the other will leave from where they are and head for the rendezvous spot."

"Do you think it's that bad?" She asked.

"I don't know, I just want to be careful. They found one of those girls, it hasn't been on the news but she's probably not the only one they found." He explained.

"Let's hope it doesn't come to that, but I'll be ready. I'll have my bags packed." She reached over and put her hand on his. He turned his palm upward and they intertwined their fingers holding one another's hand. "I love you." She said looking into his ice blue eyes. He leaned toward her, and they kissed tenderly.

"Do you want to go into the bedroom?" He asked. She stood up pulling on his hand that was still in hers. He got up and followed her into their bedroom still holding her hand. They made love. After they laid next to each other, his arm under her neck and the other across her side as she cuddled next to him with her head on his chest. "You can be so gentle with me. You make me feel so loved." She said with a tear rolling down her cheek. "I never want to be separated from you, please be careful."

"You bring out the best in me, my love. I would be lost without you. I'll always do my best to take care of you, and always be with you. You understand that don't you?" He asked.

"I have no doubt, I just worry. I know you can't help some of the problems you have and things you do. Just as I can't help the physical problems I have. We just have to be careful."

He rolled onto his side facing her. "I promise, I will be careful, and will control myself as long as I can." He lifted her chin and passionately kissed her as they made love for a second time.

Afterward he fell asleep. She slid to the side of the bed, dressed herself and went into the living room to watch television. She watched the news channels to see if there was anything that might be of importance to them, but found nothing. She knew her husband well, this was the first time he was ever the slightest concerned about their life together. Even back in 2004 he didn't even blink when that girl was discovered, so why now she wondered.

They had talked for hours over the past few years of what to do if he was ever found out. She knew the plan as if she had lived it rather than just talked about it. He believed that this time was different but she couldn't figure out why.

~ ~ ~ ~ ~ ~ ~ ~ ~ ~ ~

Jim returned from the hospital disappointed. "No one recognized the sketch. I asked everyone even people who had nothing to do with the case! I also stopped at the gas stations and corner stores, this guy is a ghost!" Jim sat down mentally exhausted, he looked at Nikki. "Sorry kiddo, I really was hoping for a lead from that sketch."

Nikki shrugged her shoulders, she too was disappointed. "It's okay."

"Also the VW did belong to the grandmother of the patient in the ICU. But she didn't see anything either. I also have a letter from the company that services the video cameras. John Sage asked them for it when they came to replace the camera that wasn't working. It states that moisture got into the camera causing it to short out. It sounds like this guy either got really lucky or somehow new the camera wasn't working. There was no evidence of it being tampered with. The guard said that John Sage specifically asked them to check for that."

"Thank you Jim. I'll make a call to my office. The tech team may be able to tell us if there was any way he could have known that the camera had malfunctioned." Daniel walked over to the phone that was on the desk to call the FBI office in Albany. He spoke to Francine Dapper who was an expert on surveillance. He had a smirk on his face when he turned back toward the group. "It seems that if he had the right equipment he could have known there was no power to the camera. Francine said that you can buy such things at a number of places and over the internet. They range in price from around one hundred dollars to the thousands depending on how sophisticated you want them to be."

"Should we go on the assumption that he would have that type of equipment at this point? I can't see how else he could have taken Suzy without being caught on camera, short of it being a coincidence, which I don't believe in." Jessica was voicing her opinion.

"I think we better, Jess." Daniel had also come to the same opinion.

"That would put this guy at a whole new level. He would have to be organized, intelligent, meticulous and patient. That's a very dangerous combination." Sounding a little unnerved Justin Forest continued. "He is going to be very hard to catch. We have never seen a serial killer with that combination of characteristics. The closest one to him would have been Jerome McEvoy. He killed six women in 2002 in New Mexico. He was finally caught after getting into a car crash in the neighborhood of his last victim, on the night she was killed. A group of teens were driving too fast and lost control around a curve sideswiping his car. He was knocked unconscious and was hospitalized. He didn't have a reason for being in that part of the neighborhood so it raised suspicion among the local police, who called us. Otherwise we would not have ever suspected him."

“So what you’re saying then is we may not find him unless something happens to expose him?” Nikki really hoped she was wrong.

“We will find him quicker if something happens, but we will still find him. We have no other choice and won’t stop until we do.” Daniel was defiant in his goal to stop whoever was doing these murders.

“I’m glad to hear that, I feel the same way.” Nikki said relieved by Daniel’s answer.

“I’m in agreement.” Added Jessica.

“I couldn’t live with myself if I stopped looking for him.” Justin added.

“This guy doesn’t know what he is in for.” Daniel proudly said looking at the team he would be leading and working with.

It was getting late and Jim was feeling a little out of place. “I better get going. Will I see you tomorrow Nikki?”

“I’ll walk you out Jim, hold on a second.” Nikki went to get her folder of paperwork she would be taking with her in the morning, then said goodnight to Jessica, Justin, and Daniel before heading out with Jim.

“We are all going to miss you. I’m still your partner here in Mackinaw you know, you can call me anytime. Take care of yourself Nikki.” Jim said in his fatherly way that made Nikki feel safe.

“I know I can depend on you Jim. I’ll keep you updated on what we find. We’re going to head to Wilkes-Barre in the morning. Then I hope we will be going to the Oak Tree Land Development Corporation to speak with the man who was at the Eastern Holiday Motel in Middletown. You really don’t have to worry about me; Jessica, Daniel and Justin are good at what they do. I feel safe with them.”

“I’ll still worry, kiddo, even though I know you’ll do great. Just don’t underestimate anyone and suspect everyone until you know the truth. Okay.”

“I’ll remember that Jim, I promise, and I’ll be back before you know it.”

Jim and Nikki hugged, he squeezed her tight. She was the daughter he never had, and she wasn’t that much older than the eldest of his two sons. He held both her hands as they parted, he then squeezed them as he let go to get into his car. He watched Nikki walk down the street to her apartment as he sat in the driver seat getting ready to turn the key. “I don’t think you’ll be back any time soon, kiddo. This is just the beginning of your career.” Jim backed out of the motel parking lot and headed home where his wife and sons were waiting for him to have dinner.

Once at her apartment, Nikki packed her suitcases and called her sister Suzanne. She wanted to make sure she would be awake at six in the morning when she would drop Cindy off. Cindy stayed with Suzanne whenever Nikki was away for a few days. Suzanne’s two daughters loved having the cat there to chase strings as they pulled them along the floor, and then jump into the air after them. Cindy also loved the attention from the two girls. Nikki knew she would be happy and safe while she was out of town.

The next morning Nikki drove to her sister's house to drop Cindy off. Suzanne then drove Nikki to the motel where she was going to meet the rest of the team. She then drove Nikki's car back with her to store it in her garage until Nikki returned.

Nikki waited in the motel lobby until the entire team was assembled. The four loaded their suitcases in the FBI van. It was now heavily laden with computers and other electronic equipment as well as their luggage. They began their five hour trip to the Wilkes-Barre area of Pennsylvania. Along the way they discussed the evidence from New York and Pennsylvania to be sure they all knew it well, and to put any questions they had to rest. They stopped for lunch in Binghamton, NY before heading over the Pennsylvania border for the last leg of their journey.

Once they arrived in Wilkes-Barre they headed to the Hawthorne Inn and booked two adjoining rooms. Nikki and Jessica shared one while Daniel and Justin settled into the other. Daniel and Justin's room would serve as their meeting area so the girls would have privacy. They each had computers in their rooms along with printers and fax machines. This was to be their home base until they left Pennsylvania.

It had been a tiring drive, and it was now late afternoon. They decided to rest and start fresh on Sunday morning. Daniel however made a few phone calls preparing the way for them on the following day. He spoke to the Wilkes-Barre Police Department so they would be expecting them and googled Oak Tree Land Development Corporation to see what he could find out about the company and the people who worked there. After that he checked the FBI files to see if anyone who worked at the corporation, or the corporation itself, had any type of record, or had ever been investigated. He found nothing. He intended to head to Allentown early in the week and speak with the local police and the Oak Tree Land Development Corporation management.

He realized it was getting late and he could see Justin stirring in his bed. He didn't want to wake him, it was time to turn off his computer and get some sleep.

~~~~~~~~~~
~~~~~~~~~~

Nikki was up early, eager to get started with the investigation. She showered and was relaxing as she waited to head down to the restaurant for breakfast once Jessica was ready. Daniel and Justin were going to meet them there at eight-thirty.

“Okay, I’m ready, are you?” Jessica asked.

“Yes, I’m eager to get going.” Nikki replied as she slipped her shoes on.

When they walked into the Hawthorne’s restaurant, Daniel and Justin were already there with coffee waiting. As they approached the table Daniel looked up. “Hey guys the coffee just arrived it’s nice and hot.”

Seeing the girls sit down the waitress came over with menus. After a few minutes she returned to take their order. Holding her pad and pen ready to write the waitress asked. “What can I bring you?”

They each gave their order; the waitress then refilled their coffees before leaving.

Daniel looked away from the waitress and toward the other three. "I worked up an appetite last night after the rest of you went to bed. I spoke with the sergeant here in Wilkes-Barre; they will be expecting us this morning. I also did a little research on the Oak Tree Land Development Corporation. I found the names of the top people there and ran them and the company through the FBI VICAP. They came through without a blemish."

Justin noticed the look on Jessica and Nikki's faces and felt he needed to add to what Daniel was saying. "They very well could be on the up and up, and their employee could just have been in New York on business. Or he could be our killer, we won't know until we check them all out."

"That's true; everyone is clean until they get caught." Daniel added laughing.

The waitress brought their breakfast. Their food was cooked perfectly and they ate in almost complete silence.

When she was finished Nikki excused herself to go to the ladies room, Jessica went with her. “I don’t want to have to find a bathroom once we get going.”

“I know what you mean, Nikki, who knows when we’ll get another chance.”

They returned to the table just as the waitress was taking the plates and leaving the check. Daniel picked the check up and went to pay while the other three went out to the van.

“Are we ready for some crime solving?” Daniel asked as he got into the van. “After that delicious breakfast I think I could catch anyone. It was a great way to start the day.”

They all agreed as they pulled out of the parking lot and headed down the road to the police station. It was three miles away according to the GPS, all downhill. The roadway was so steep Nikki felt like she was in a plane heading for its final approach to the runway. She saw the signs for the runaway truck stop along the road and wondered how often they were used.

Once they reached the valley they drove the last mile through the town before pulling into the parking lot of the police station. Nikki looked over the station, it was fairly new. There was only one patrol car in the lot, probably one or two more were out on patrol. It seemed to be about the same size as her station back in Mackinaw.

Once they entered the station Daniel spoke to the officer at the window. “Good morning, my name is Daniel Dillon. My colleagues and I are here to go over the murder case of Nancy Walnick.”

“Oh, yes, you’re from the FBI. The night sergeant told me you would be coming in. I’ll buzz you in through the door to your left.”

When he heard the buzz sound Justin opened the door allowing the other three to enter before him. They followed the desk sergeant to a room in the back of the office where two boxes were sitting on a table. “This is all the information on that case, if you need anything I’ll be at the window.”

“Thank you, I’m sure we’ll be fine.” Daniel answered as he took the lid off of the first box.

Justin pulled the second box toward him and took the lid off that one also. Inside both were folders with dates and names on them, along with clear plastic bags that contained various articles of clothing, a cell phone, and jewelry.

Daniel handed Nikki a few folders and motioned at Justin to do the same with Jessica.

“Read through what you have, if you find anything different from what we have discussed, or notice anything that sparks your interest give a shout.” Daniel would be surprised if they found anything different but wanted to make sure. “Whoever finds the cell phone records give a yell. I’m curious to see if the call Nancy received was a burner phone. If so maybe there will be information on who purchased it.”

After two hours Justin spoke up. “Eureka! I have the phone records!”

They all gathered around to look at the paper Justin was holding. Justin ran his finger down the dates till he got to September 18th. "Nancy received five calls that day, the last two were calls from family, probably looking for her. The third is a call that lasted less than five minutes, but it looks like she answered it."

"Is there anything that looks like they did a trace on the phone?" Jessica asked.

"Not that I see." Justin said as he looked through the papers that followed the phone records.

"You three keep looking. I'm going to talk to the investigating officer if he or she is still around." Daniel took the phone records and headed down the hall. "Sergeant." He called. "Is the investigating officer available to talk to us?"

"That would be Captain Murphy, Janelle Murphy. She works the night shift this week; she will be in around eleven tonight. I could get you her number. She's probably asleep right now but you could try her later this afternoon." The desk sergeant replied.

"Yes, thank you. Were you around in 2004?" Daniel asked the sergeant.

"No, I started in 2008. But I remember when the murder happened. The captain was a sergeant at the time. She and two other officers worked the case, they were in the news almost daily for awhile. Mark Gould retired a year later and has since passed away, but Larry Enrish is still around. He should be in soon, he works the evening shift. He became a detective once the force grew big enough to have detectives."

After getting Captain Murphy's number, Daniel thanked the sergeant and returned to inform the other three what he had learned.

"How far have we gotten on those boxes of files?" Daniel asked.

"Almost through them." Justin answered.

"Good. Justin can you and Jessica stay here and finish going through the boxes, and then speak with a Larry Enrish? He'll be coming in for the evening shift in about an hour and a half? He was one of the investigators in Nancy's murder. I want to have

Nikki go with me to the site where the body was found and just have a look around."

Justin and Jessica agreed.

"I also have the number of the lead investigator. She works the graveyard shift, we can give her a call later today. We need to know if they had anything more on the phone calls, as well as anything they may not have put into the files. Also see if Nancy's cell phone will be able to be charged somehow." Daniel was all business; he was on the hunt and had a scent.

"No problem, Daniel. If you're not back when we're done we'll get a ride and meet you back at the motel." Justin answered for the two of them.

Daniel and Nikki headed out to the van. Nikki found him easy to talk to and was relaxed around him. That was unusual for her. Usually she would find herself nervous around men that she found attractive. She would find it difficult to have a conversation without being extremely self-conscious, especially if they were in authority.

"This is beautiful country, it reminds me a little of New York. The mountains aren't quite as tall, and that crispness the Adirondacks have isn't here. It has warmth about it though." Nikki remarked as she looked out the van window.

The GPS in the van announced that it would be eight hundred yards till the next turn off Mountain Road. "At the end of this road is where we get out. According to the report she was found about half a mile up the trail after the road's end."

Daniel and Nikki began walking down the trail; it was well worn by hikers and isolated from view. "This looks eerily familiar." Nikki commented. "This guy is the outdoor type, the area is very similar to where Suzy was found."

"Yea, it is. I think coming here has given us more insight into this guy. He's not a city dweller that's for sure." Daniel remarked. "According to the hand drawn map from the case, the spot is right up ahead. There should be a large rock, a couple oak trees and a decline off to the right."

"That looks like the rock there, and there is a decline to the right." Nikki sped up her gait to look down the incline. Holding onto one of the oak trees for support she peered down to see brush consisting of Mountain Laurel and other wild plants.

Standing next to Nikki, Daniel pointed. "To the left there, do you see the smaller rocks near that little trickling brook? That's where Nancy's body was found."

They stood staring at the spot and the surrounding area. "This is definitely his style." Nikki was taking the area in, getting a feel for it and him.

"We have a nice profile of this guy so far." Daniel explained as they headed out of the woodland and back to the van. "Coming here made him clearer to me. He enjoys the outdoors, specifically the country and isolation. We aren't going to find him living in the city or even a small town."

"I can see that too. He likes the mountains. I would take a chance and say he probably lives within a fifty mile radius of here. Nancy was killed nine years ago, the desk clerk back in Middletown said he was around thirty-two or three. That would make him near twenty-three or four when he murdered Nancy."

"Keep going Nikki, what else." Daniel wanted to hear what Nikki was thinking.

"I would find it hard to believe Nancy was the first woman he murdered. It doesn't feel right that she would have been. So that makes me wonder how many others there are, and when exactly he began killing!"

"That is a good question, and I agree, she was not the first. All the evidence from this case points to experience on his part."

"The one question I have is that in New York there were three bodies at the site where we found Suzy. Here there was just one. Did they look the area over for others? If Nancy was the only one here then why did he place three victims together in New York?" Nikki was confused by this.

"All good questions. I'm not sure how thorough they looked the area over since Nancy was the only one missing. They weren't looking for anyone else. I'm puzzled by there being three bodies in New York too. Returning to the same spot seems odd for this guy, too much of a risk. According to Jill and Mary, the two hikers that saw him, he didn't linger in the area. He was in and out pretty quick, so he wasn't checking on the other two." Daniel was trying to get into the mind of this guy, but he was having difficulty with the inconsistencies. They would make it hard to pinpoint patterns to this guy's behavior in the future.

Once in the van they headed back down Mountain Road and across the Susquehanna River to the center of Wilkes-Barre. Nikki was making notes about the site where Nancy's body was found in the notebook they had in the van. She also read some of the notes left by other members of the team. It was a place where they could reflect and jot down ideas so nothing would be lost or forgotten.

"Nikki, can you give Justin a call and see if they are still at the station, and if they spoke to Larry Enrish?" Daniel asked.

"Sure." Nikki took her phone out of her pocket and dialed Justin. "Hi, it's Nikki. Have you been able to speak to Larry Enrish and are you and Jessica at the station or motel?" … "Okay, Daniel and I will be there shortly. Bye." Nikki turned to Daniel. "They are still at the station. Larry Enrish had nothing new to add, but he said something else came up."

They arrived at the station five minutes later. When they entered Jessica and Justin were waiting anxious to share what they had found.

"What's going on?" Daniel asked as he and Nikki walked toward them.

"It looks like Nancy wasn't the only one. We finished with the boxes and began looking at other unsolved murders while we were waiting. Jessica noticed a case from 1998." Justin started the conversation.

"I wasn't looking for anything to be connected with the case that we're working on. I was just browsing through the unsolved murder files when I noticed the details of one particular case. She was twenty-one and was found by hunters in the fall of 1998. According to the report from the coroner she had been in the forest about two years. So she was murdered in 1996, the only thing that was left were her bones. The cause of death was listed as multiple stab wounds determined by the marks they found on some of the bones."

"What was her name?" Nikki asked.

"Deborah Weaver. She was a college student who went missing in the summer of 1996. It says that she was traveling with college friends. They were going to vacation in Lancaster, visit the Amish sites and head out to Hershey Park before returning to the University of Virginia in August. She was found less than a half mile from where Nancy was found!" Jessica was reading over the file attached to the coroner's report.

"They must be connected. Are there any details about the stab wounds, like location or type of blade used?" Nikki asked.

"The coroner's report doesn't get very specific. But it states that the wounds were in the torso. I would say that this was done by our perp, until we prove otherwise." Jessica added.

"Who was the coroner?" Daniel wanted to go and speak with him.

"Johnson Smithers." Jessica read the typed name at the bottom of the report.

"Justin, will you come with me to see Johnson Smithers? Jess and Nikki, can one of you continue to go through the files and the other contact Deborah Weaver's family to see if they can add anything?"

They both nodded in agreement.

"If you don't mind Nikki, I'll keep looking through the files, I have a feel for them."

"Sure, Jess, where's the number for the family?" Nikki asked.

Jessica handed her the copy of the file that she made. "Do they know you made a copy?"

"No, I thought it better if I didn't ask!" The two giggled as they went about their assignments.

Two hours later Daniel and Justin returned to the station. "We met with Johnson and he said that he definitely remembered that case. He remembered because it was the first murder case he ever had to do an autopsy on. He confirmed the stab wounds were identical to

Suzy and the other victims. How did it go with the two of you?" Daniel inquired.

"I didn't find any other victims that fit our perps profile." Jessica answered.

"I spoke to Deborah's parents. They didn't know any more than what was in the file. But her mother gave me the number of her college roommate. She was the last one to see her. When I called her, she said that she and Deborah were at a gift shop when Deborah received a call and said she would be back. She said that she had to call her mother right away, and needed privacy. Something about her brother being in trouble. She went to the car while her roommate finished paying for the t-shirt she was purchasing. When the roommate went out to the car, Deborah was nowhere to be found. Sounds familiar doesn't it!" Nikki remarked.

"He already had his pattern down back in 1996. So when did he start killing?" Justin wondered out loud.

"I would take a chance and say in his late teens or early 20's. Think about it. At twenty-seven he is confident and has a pattern in place which hasn't changed very much since then. We have not found any victims that show signs of him being unsure or sloppy. When we find a victim that shows that, we will know when he began. It's with those victims that we'll be able to find him. That'll be where he left evidence. I only hope we recognize those victims when we see them. It was quite awhile ago, almost twenty years, and they may seem very different at first glance."

Daniel had a strange look about him, Nikki thought as she was watching and listening to what he was saying. He was nervous, something about this guy was unnerving to him. She looked away when Daniel looked at her and their eyes met. She didn't want him to think she was starring or saw anything in him that looked like weakness.

Daniel continued. "Let's head back to the motel and get a good night's sleep. Tomorrow we'll head over to the Oak Tree Land Development Corporation where our suspect works."

They headed to the van after thanking the Wilkes-Barre Police Department for their cooperation. As they were walking Daniel approached Nikki. "I saw you looking through me back there. What were you thinking?"

Caught off guard by his being unashamed and straightforwardness, Nikki answered. "Wow, I don't quite know what to say. You just looked a little unnerved or upset, that's all."

"The truth is Nikki, I have hunted and caught over a dozen killers during my career. Half during my days as a state trooper and half as an FBI agent hunting serial killers. This one is different, I can feel it. He's not typical. He has a profile, but my gut is telling me that it's not going to be enough to catch him."

"How will we find his earliest murders? Even Deborah didn't show up with VICAP, and she fits the profile." Nikki said as she and Daniel had stopped walking and were talking on the side walk. Jessica and Justin had crossed the parking lot to the van.

"All I can think is that she wasn't entered into the system. If local authorities don't get on board with placing information in the system this is what happens." Daniel sounded matter of fact with his explanation.

"We'll have a hard time finding them then, if we ever can."

"Don't sound so defeated Nikki, there are ways. Time consuming ways, but none the less, ways to find them."

Justin pulled the van up next to the side walk, Daniel and Nikki went around to the far side and got in. "Nikki brought up a valid point." Daniel began, "We need to find the perp's first victims. Other than calling every police station in Pennsylvania and New York, any suggestions?" Daniel knew that the two of them would be curious about his and Nikki's conversation. He wanted to control the way that they would hear what they were speaking about. The last thing he wanted was for them to hear what Nikki had seen in him. So he steered the conversation in the direction of the perpetrator.

Nikki noticed his deliberate evasion of the details of their conversation, and chose to keep his secret.

On the drive back to the motel they bounced ideas off of one another on how to best locate the killer's original victims. They decided to call locally around Wilkes-Barre and to the other towns nearby as well as checking the archives at the newspaper. They would also try speaking with the state police centering on unsolved murders from fifteen to twenty years ago.

Once back in their room Nikki and Jessica put on the television to watch local news, weather and whatever else of interest they could find. They both enjoyed sleeping with the television on and their favorite shows were comedies, something to make them laugh and keep their thoughts off of the details of their jobs.

Jessica fell asleep early.

Nikki was having trouble sleeping and decided to think about the case. She opened her briefcase and took out the sketch of their suspect. She lay in bed staring at him, black hair and blue eyes. She thought it sounded like he may be Irish, or at least have ancestors from that area. She thought of how Daniel spoke of him, the slight tremble in his voice that could barely be detected. She realized Daniel was afraid of him and it was taking a lot for him to hide that fact. But why would he be afraid? Nikki pondered as she continued to memorize the sketch. Justin said he was smart, not just smart, very intelligent. She knew Daniel believed they would eventually catch him; maybe it's the hunt he's worried about. She finally fell asleep.

While asleep she dreamt of the man in the sketch. As she was hunting him, he was in turn hunting her. She could tell that he could feel her presence, and was aware of her thoughts. That's why he was always one step ahead of her at every turn. In her dream she was frustrated, and angry at the same time. She woke in a cold sweat and glanced over at Jessica who was sleeping soundly. She put the sketch back into her briefcase and relaxed watching television until she fell back to sleep.

CHAPTER NINE

She was weeding her garden when he awoke and came looking for her. He saw her leaning over in the vegetable garden and walked toward her. “How is everything growing?”

“Not too bad, the tomatoes will need to be staked soon. This has been a good year so far. Your idea of planting early and putting little greenhouses over them is working out nicely.”

She stood and gave him a hug and quick kiss on the lips. “Can I make you anything to eat sweetheart?”

“No, not right now. I was thinking of taking a ride into town, do you want to come with me?”

“Sure, I need to buy a couple of things. I have to wash up first though.”

“Do you want to get breakfast at the diner, we haven’t done that in awhile?” He asked.

“Yes, that sounds good. I would like that.” She said as she walked into the house then down the hall to the bathroom. She washed her face and brushed her hair and teeth. As she went to their room to put on fresh clothes she noticed her husband standing outside. He was leaning against the large maple tree in the front yard with his arm outstretched, as if he was keeping the tree from falling over. His head was down like he was watching something on the ground. She could tell something was bothering him. She had known him for twenty some years and he was always the same, his personality was light, joking at times. The last few days he was quiet, burdened. She finished getting dressed and went outside to the car where her husband was now sitting in the driver seat waiting.

"Sorry I took so long." She said.

"Your fine dear, I'm not in a hurry." He said as he turned the car around and drove down the driveway.

"What's bothering you? You haven't been yourself the last few days."

"I don't really know how to explain it. But I believe we need to leave soon. I feel it, I dream about someone hunting us, tracking us." He hit the steering wheel with the palm of his hand, startling his wife. “Sorry, Hun.” He reached over and held her hand. “It isn’t you, it could never be you. You’re the best thing that ever happened to me. I’ll do whatever I can to keep you out of this. I promise.” He squeezed her hand before placing his back on the steering wheel to navigate the winding roads down the hillside and into the valley.

He pulled up to the diner in Knowlton, the closest town to where they lived. They sat in silence for a few minutes. “I’ll do whatever you want, go wherever you say. Just keep yourself safe, however you have to.” She took her seat belt off and turned sideways in her seat so she could look at him.

He hesitated then looked over at her. “I may have to separate from you for awhile, not right away, and hopefully never. But if it comes down to it, I will have to be alone to keep us both safe. I’m sorry. I don’t want you to think I don’t love you. Do you understand that?”

She felt her eyes tearing and looked away so he wouldn't see. "It'll be hard. I hope it doesn't come to that either. If it does I'll wait for you."

Neither could look at the other as they sat silent in the car for a few more minutes. He opened his door first, as they got out of the SUV and went into the diner.

They rarely went into town and didn't know anyone there, nor did anyone there recognize them as living nearby. He liked it that way. She was happy with her life also, and had no need for companionship outside of her husband.

They walked into the diner and sat at a booth by the window. As they waited for a waitress to take their order they read over the menu. "What looks good to you dear?" He asked, as if they were just regular people out for breakfast and the conversation they just had never took place.

"I think I'll have an omelet, how about you?"

"Steak and eggs sounds good this morning. Are you having coffee?"

"No, hot chocolate I think."

They put their menus down and the waitress came over to take their order. They ate and then left the diner to head over to the hardware store. She needed tomato stakes and chicken feed. He needed a pair of work gloves and oil for the lawn mower. They put their purchases in the trunk of the car and decided to take a walk through town.

The town of Knowlton was about twenty miles northwest of Wilkes-Barre, nestled between three mountains. Route 6 passed through the center of town and there were large maple trees on either side of the road. The Main Street and sidewalk was cobblestone in the oldest parts of the town, along with a few of the side streets. The street lights were single black thick poles with swirl designs up and down the sides. The light on top was covered by an octagon globe. He enjoyed the quaint feel of the town. It reminded him of simpler times, when he was different, before he was fifteen and started to be haunted by the dark desires from deep inside him.

They walked hand in hand, taking their time, window shopping as they passed by the stores along Main Street. They strolled three blocks to the town park and sat on a bench. Pigeons were walking around cooing and bobbing their heads, looking for something to eat. The town had a medium sized fountain that had a soothing rhythmic sound as the water came out the top and over the sides. It was a beautiful spring day the sun was warm and felt good. He wanted to remember this day with his wife. He had a feeling it may be one of the last untroubled days he would have for some time.

~~~~~~~~~~

Monday morning came too fast. Nikki was on the tired side from not getting a good night's sleep. She brought an extra cup of coffee with her as they began the drive to Allentown. It wasn't far, a little over an hour, taking route 476 traveling south-east from Wilkes-Barre.

"What are we going to do if they don't cooperate with us?" Jessica asked Daniel.
~~~~~~~~~~

“Then I will have to make a few calls and find a judge to give us a warrant. I don’t think they’ll be able to resist my charm though.” Daniel joked to lighten the mood.

“Justin will you read the history of the Oak Tree Land Development Corporation please. This way we will all be on the same page.” Daniel asked.

“It was started about twenty years ago by Matthew Newman. They purchase large plots of undeveloped land, portion them into lots and resell the lots for development. There has been no real complaints against them, they have high ratings, and are considered a good company to do business with. The company’s owner retired five years ago, his oldest son runs it now. His name is Matt Newman. He’s forty-two, is married with a daughter who is eighteen years old. He graduated from Penn State with a degree in business and as far as we can tell has never been in any trouble.”

“How hands on is he, does it say?” Jessica asked.

“According to this he is very involved in the business end of the company, overseeing the expanding of the company out west in

Ohio and Missouri. He gets reports from the VP and other managers at bi-weekly meetings. He doesn't deal with the individual sales of the land or the purchasing of the land. His younger brother Jason is the Vice President and he directly oversees both of those areas."

"So he must be the boss of our perp." Nikki commented.

"Yea, it looks that way. They have quite a few "scouts," as they refer to them. They go to different parts of the country to look at land the company is interested in purchasing. If it looks promising they finalize the purchase. From there the managers under Jason Newman take it and divide the land and put it up for resale. Our suspect is one of the scouts. Interestingly they rarely even come to the office. They communicate with cell phones and emails."

"Well, how perfect of a job for our perp! It fits what we know of him so far." Nikki commented.

"Yes, it certainly does." Added Daniel.

The GPS announced 'you have reached your destination' as Daniel turned onto Sumner Avenue.

"This must be the place." Daniel remarked as he pulled into the parking lot.

"Not a shabby place is it!" Justin was noticing the immaculate landscaping and the exterior of the building. It was a single story building with white and grey stone and large tinted windows.

"Looks like the gangs all here." Jessica said pointing to the parking spaces labeled CEO and VP which were occupied by a couple of very nice vehicles.

After parking the van they entered the building. It was lit by natural light coming in through skylights. Small trees and plants were planted along a walkway that led to the front desk. A single receptionist sat behind the desk. "Can I help you?" She asked.

"You certainly can." Daniel replied. "We would like to speak to Jason Newman."

"Do you have an appointment?" She asked.

"No, we don't."

"Okay, let me see if he is available."

The receptionist picked up the phone to call Jason. Daniel listened out of one ear while he pretended to converse with the rest of his team.

"He'll be right down. The waiting area is over to the right, you can have a seat if you would like."

"Thank you." Daniel said as he and the other three walked over to the waiting area. It was as nice as the rest of the reception area. A saltwater fish tank was on the far wall and a large screen TV hung in the corner next to it. Plants, tables and chairs lined the walls on either side.

After ten minutes a man approached them wearing a suit and tie. "Hello, I'm Jason Newman, what can I do for you?"

The team stood up. Daniel approached Jason and shook his hand as he introduced himself. "My name is Daniel Dillon. This is my team Justin, Jessica and Nikki." Daniel pulled out his credentials. "We're with the FBI and we need some information about one of your employees."

“Have they done something wrong?” He asked with a slight tremble in his voice.

“We believe he may be a witness to a crime without realizing it.” Daniel felt it best no to point a finger of guilt just yet.

“Who is it you are looking for?”

“We don’t have a name, only a sketch from another witness.” Daniel reached into his briefcase and pulled out a sketch of the perp.

“He was recently in Middletown, New York.” Daniel showed the sketch to Jason.

“I don’t recognize him. However if he is one of our scouts I wouldn’t see him often, if at all. Let me look and see if I can find out who was in that area recently. You can come with me to my office.” Jason led them down a hall to his office. He took out three files. “These are the men who have been in New York.” He looked at each one, then took out a picture from a folder. “This could be him? His name is Lobo Dylan.”

Daniel took the picture and the other three leaned over his shoulder to see the picture. "What do you think?" He asked the team.

"That looks a lot like the sketch, younger though." Jessica said.

"Is this a recent photo?" Daniel asked.

"It was taken when he was hired, that was almost ten years ago." Jason replied.

"Do you have an address?" Daniel hoped he would continue to cooperate.

"Yes, it's in Altoona. I would say that it's about three and a half hours west of here."

"Can you write that down for me please?" Daniel felt like leaping into the air with joy over this new information, it seemed almost too easy.

"Here you go, I hope he can help. He should be there till Monday of next week. After that he is due to head to Virginia."

"Thank you, we appreciate the cooperation." Daniel said, the other three also thanked him as Jason showed them out.

Once in the van they let out their feelings of achievement. "That was so much easier than I expected." Daniel exclaimed. "I was prepared for a battle, what a letdown!"

"We should head to Altoona. Could it be this easy, it just seems too easy, ya know?" Justin added.

"I wonder if he was ever in Virginia before." Nikki chimed in.

"What a spoiler, Nikki." Jessica said laughing and tapping her on the arm.

"She's right even though it does spoil the mood. We'll have to add Virginia to our areas of interest in this case. He may have killed there also." Daniel commented.

"Let's eat and then head to Altoona this afternoon. What do you say?" Daniel asked.

"Let's get drive thru, so we don't lose any time?" Nikki added.

They all agreed. Daniel put the address he was given into the GPS. "We can take I80 west and get there in three hours and twenty five minutes. That will put us there about two-thirty or three this afternoon."

"I don't know any other way I would rather spend the day!" Justin remarked.

They went through the drive thru of the first fast food restaurant they saw, and then headed west.

Three and a half hours later they were in Altoona heading down Beverly Blvd. "That's the house over there." Justin pointed to a dark blue home with white shutters. It had a porch with a few chairs. Flower boxes with dead flowers from the year before and a wooden fence that went around each side to the back.

"I'll drive around the block and then pull up in front." Daniel wondered if anyone had called to warn him after they left the Development Corporation.

No one spoke as they went to the front door and knocked. A dog barked and they could hear a male voice call. "I'll get it."

The door opened revealing a medium sized black poodle and a teenage boy. “Can I help you?” He asked.

“Yes, we are looking for Lobo Dylan, is he here?” Daniel asked.

“That’s my dad, hold on he’s out back.”

The boy walked back into the house calling, “Dad, it’s for you.”

Daniel mouthed the word dad and had a questioning look on his face.

A minute later an older man came to the door. “Hello, what can I do for you?” He was in his late fifties, had salt and pepper hair, blue eyes and was about six feet tall. The team realized he was not who they were looking for.

“My name is Daniel Dillon, I work for the FBI. This is my team Justin, Jessica, and Nikki. We were given this address from the employer of Lobo Dylan; but he would be half your age.”

“My name is Lobo Dylan, but you’re probably looking for my oldest son. Come in and have a seat.”

They entered the house and followed Mr. Dylan to the kitchen. "Would you like something to drink?"

"Do you have anything cold?" Daniel asked.

"We have ice tea or water." He said as he opened the refrigerator door.

He took out five glasses and filled each one with each person's request. Then sat down with a glass of iced tea before speaking. "Why are you looking for Lobo?"

"We want to ask him a few questions. He may be a witness in a case we're working on." Daniel stuck with the same line he had used at his employer.

"I haven't seen him in about fifteen years. I threw him out of my house when he turned eighteen. I had nothing but trouble from that one. We gave him everything, he wanted for nothing and yet it was never enough. Once he broke the law he was out of here. I have two other children to raise and they didn't need his influence."

“So you have no idea where he is then?” Daniel continued.

“No, I don’t. But whatever the reason you’re looking for him, he probably did it.”

Mrs. Dylan came in the back door as he ended his sentence.

“Oh, hello. I didn’t know we had company.” She was startled by their presence.

“Hello Mrs. Dylan, we were looking for your oldest son. But your husband was saying he doesn’t live here.” Daniel looked carefully to see her reaction.

“Oh, he left here many years ago. Why do you need him?” She asked.

“He might be a witness in an investigation, we’re from the FBI.” Daniel told her.

“I wish we could help you, but he doesn’t keep in touch with us.” Mrs. Dylan replied.

She sounded as though she would like to see him, unlike her husband, Daniel thought. “Can you tell me about him? What kind of trouble was he in as a youth?” Daniel inquired.

Mr. Dylan answered. “At first he was just curious. He would get into everything, take apart radios, old toasters things like that. He was always smarter than other children his age and didn’t really have anything in common with them. He had a hard time making friends. But as he got older he just didn’t realize his boundaries, and he had no respect for others’ boundaries. If he wanted something he would just take it. He stole constantly. When he was fifteen it was obvious something was wrong, he was just a bad seed. That was the year he changed for the worse. We had no control over him after that. I threw him out when he was eighteen when the local police came looking for him. He had bullied a few local boys, when they reported him they said they feared for their safety. I hoped that he would straighten out after that, but he never did.”

“Did he ever hurt anyone or an animal?” Justin asked.

"No, he wasn't violent. The only reason he even threatened those boys was because they had said something to one of the local girls. I believe it was the sister of his friend. She was the only real friend he ever had. I suppose he felt he had to protect her sister." Mrs. Dylan explained.

"What was her name?" Jessica asked.

"Do you remember, hun?" Mr. Dylan passed the question to his wife.

"Elizabeth McMurray, I believe. It's a sad story, her father was an alcoholic and they were such a poor family. He couldn't hold down a job and her mother was in and out of the hospital for depression. She seemed like a nice girl, he brought her around a few times." Mrs. Dylan was troubled by the questions they were asking. "Do you suspect him of something?" She asked.

"We only want to question him, to find out what he knows, if anything." Daniel explained.

"Where is this girl now?" Jessica asked wondering if she wasn't a victim.

"She was badly injured in a car crash shortly after Lobo left home. It was her father's fault. I know she was disabled after that due to her injuries. But I don't think she lives around here anymore." Mrs. Dylan explained.

"Can you tell us where she lived? We would like to talk to one of her family members." Jessica hoped that they knew where she was.

"She lived on 24th street, near 10th. I don't know the house number but it's green with a hedge of bushes around the front yard."

"Lobo is an unusual name, is it a family name?" Nikki inquired.

"Yes, the first born men in my family have had that name for generations." Mr. Dylan explained.

They finished their drinks and then left to speak with Elizabeth's family. The house wasn't hard to find. They approached the door and knocked.

An older man answered the door. "Can I help you?"

“We’re from the FBI. Are you Elizabeth McMurray’s family?” Jessica asked the man who was not quite as old as he looked.

“She’s my daughter, is she alright?” He asked, concerned for her.

“As far as we know she’s fine. We were curious about her relationship with a Lobo Dylan.” Jessica explained.

“What has he done now? He never was any good. He poisoned her against us and then took her away.” Mr. McMurray said in disgust.

“Away, what do you mean?” Jessica asked.

“We were in an accident and she was hurt pretty bad. He came and took her, I haven’t seen her since. It broke her mother’s heart.” Mr. McMurray answered leaving out how he was responsible for the accident.

“So she hasn’t been in touch with you all these years?” Jessica asked.

“No, like I said he turned her against us. The only person who hears from her is our other daughter, Loretta. She lives in Duncansville.”

“Would you mind giving us your daughter’s number, we would like to find out where Elizabeth is.” Jessica explained.

“Sure, hold on.” He went to a desk across the room and pulled a book out of the drawer. He opened the book and wrote the number on a piece of paper, then headed back to the door. “There you go, if you find Elizabeth tell her to call her mother. That’s the least she could do.”

“Thank you Mr. McMurray, I will relay your message.” Jessica took the piece of paper then headed away from the door as the rest of the team followed.

“No wonder she never calls him!” Jessica whispered when they were away from the house.

They drove away in silence. Thinking about what they had heard from the two families. Daniel pulled into a gas station to fill up the van. As he got out he looked at Jessica. "Give Elizabeth's sister a call while I pump the gas."

Jessica dialed the number Mr. McMurray had given her. "Hello, my name is Jessica Lewis, I work with the FBI. Is this Loretta?" … "Do you have a few minutes to speak with me?" … "I just came from your father's house. He told us that you have had contact with your sister Elizabeth. Is that correct?" … "Would you be able to tell me where she lives?" Jessica listened to Loretta for a few minutes. "Do you have a number that I could reach her at?" … "When was the last time you spoke with your sister?" … "Do you know if she keeps in contact with a Lobo Dylan from your hometown?" Jessica looked shocked as she listened to Loretta. "That's a big help, thank you Loretta. Bye."

Daniel had finished filling the van with gas and waited for Jessica to finish her conversation before starting the van. Seeing the look on her face he waited.

Jessica put her phone down and looked at the rest of the team. "Elizabeth is Lobo's wife, they've been married for fourteen years!"

Daniel pulled the van into a parking space. "What did her sister say?"

"She doesn't know where she lives and doesn't know her phone number. All she knows is that she lives in Pennsylvania. Elizabeth calls her a couple of times a year, usually holidays and her birthday. She called in March for her birthday, they talked about an hour. Loretta said she is doing well and is happy." Jessica's disappointment showed in her voice.

"I'm really confused right now." Nikki confessed. "This guy doesn't fit the profile of a serial killer. Could we be wrong about him as a suspect?" Nikki spoke out loud what they were all thinking.

"I want to talk to the local authorities, to see what really went on when he was a teenager." Daniel redirected the conversation.

They arrived at the Altoona Police Department fifteen minutes later. Daniel took the lead. "Hello, my name is Daniel Dillon, my team and I work for the FBI. We have a few questions about someone who lived in your town sixteen years ago."

"Let me get the captain." The woman at the front desk said as she stood and walked into a room behind her.

She emerged from the room and called for Daniel and the team to come over to where she was. When they walked into the room an officer came from behind a desk. "I'm Captain Hickory, what can I do for you."

Daniel introduced himself and his team. "We're here to inquire about a man who grew up in Altoona. We spoke with his father earlier today and he said he had some troubles with the local authorities. His name is Lobo Dylan."

"Yes, I remember him. I had just made detective. He was a suspect in the disappearance of a teenage girl. We never could prove anything though. His girlfriend said he was with her when the girl disappeared. The case never went anywhere and the girl has never been found. He left town with the same girlfriend three years later and we never heard any more about him."

"Why was he a suspect?" Daniel asked.

"It seems that before the girl disappeared she told her friends that he had been following her, and that he scared her. He denied any involvement, we had nothing to go on, and he had an alibi. Although we felt the girlfriend was lying for him."

"So he was how old, fifteen or sixteen?" Daniel was trying to do the math in his head.

"Fifteen." The captain answered.

"That's young, was he ever in trouble before that?" Daniel was trying to put things together.

"Nothing serious. During our investigation we found out he had been suspected of taking a few things from the school, some sports equipment, I believe. That was it, we found no reason to charge him. He had no other problems after that, and then he left town."

"His father said that he had threatened another boy. That it had been reported to the police and that he threw him out of the house after that." Daniel questioned to see if the father's information was correct.

"Oh, yea, that's right. We had a report from two of the local boys. Well they were eighteen and nineteen at the time. They came in one afternoon and said that Lobo threatened them. Apparently they had no idea why. We went to check out their story and found out they had been tormenting a local girl. Lobo found them later and told them they wouldn't be bothering anyone again if they didn't stop. Evidently they took him seriously. We felt it was all talk since he had no past violent incidents. We did go to his house and spoke with his father because he wasn't home."

"Was Elizabeth McMurray the girl that the boys were bothering?" Jessica asked.

"No it was her sister, Loretta. She had a bad reputation back then and the two boys were following her around making inappropriate remarks. They never bothered her again after that."

"Can you give us their names? We're curious why they reacted that way. It was two against one wasn't it?" Daniel asked.

"Yes. The one boy moved away after college, the other ended up going into the service. He was wounded and now lives at the long term care facility on 18th street, his name is James Long."

"Thank you captain, you have been very helpful." Daniel shook the captain's hand and they headed back to the van.

It was a few blocks to the facility where James Long lived. The nurse on duty took them to James's room.

"You have a few guests James." The nurse said as she knocked and opened his door.

Inside was a man in a wheelchair. He was missing both legs below the knees. "Hello, to what do I owe this pleasure? I haven't had so many visitors since my last birthday."

Daniel introduced himself and the team and then asked. "Do you remember Lobo Dylan?"

James looked at them with a blank stare. “I haven’t heard that name for a long time. I knew of him.”

“We’re looking for him. The captain of the police mentioned you and a friend had a run in with him when you were in your late teens, is that right?” Daniel asked.

“Yes, we did. We were punk kids back then. We thought it would be funny to harass this girl who had a bad rep. She got pretty upset, we really felt bad about it. A couple days later Lobo came up to us at the ice cream shop, he gave us the creeps, told us we wouldn’t be around to harass anyone else if we did it again. I believed him. You should have seen the look in his eyes. The cops thought we over reacted. That was about it. He left town not too long after that with the sister of the girl, from what I heard.”

“If you remember or hear anything else, here’s my card, give us a call.” Daniel handed him a card with his number on it.

“Okay, I will.” James put the card in his shirt pocket as Daniel and the team turned and left his room.

CHAPTER TEN

They arrived back at the motel in Wilkes-Barre at ten-thirty that evening. “I’m going to head into the lounge for a drink, does anyone want to join me?” Daniel announced.

The all agreed and followed Daniel to a booth in the back. Daniel and Justin went to the bar to order drinks as Nikki and Jessica sat silently watching the television that was hanging on the wall across from them.

A few minutes later when Daniel and Justin returned, they all drank down their first drinks quickly as if they were drinking water on a hot day. They needed to quench the effects of the day’s revelations, or lack of. Nikki and Jessica decided they would go and get the second round of drinks. By the time they returned the first round was starting to have its desired effect. Nikki felt a little more relaxed and freer to say what was on her mind.

“I’m really confused by this guy. One minute he’s this cold blooded monster, the next he’s a knight in shining armor. How do you wrap your mind around that?" Nikki had opened the floodgates without realizing it.

"I've never seen inconsistencies that have such a pendulous swing in a personality! What do you do with this as a profile? I'll admit it, I'm at a loss!" Jessica seemed unwound by the day's developments.

Justin was next to say what was on his mind. "I think we need to look at the money. Now that we have names for him and his wife, we can find out where they live and who knows what else?"

"Should we even bother? Maybe we should start looking in another direction. This guy is odd but he really doesn't fit the profile of a cold blooded killer." Jessica said running her hand across her forehead, then through her hair. She wasn't a drinker, and now that she was almost done her second glass of wine she was really starting to feel a little woozy.

"Hold on Jess, this is our guy. We found out today who his first victim was. When he was fifteen years old he must have killed that missing girl." Nikki was interrupted by Justin. "What do you mean, his first victim? How do you know that?"

"You remember Justin, the girl who disappeared that said he was following her. He killed her." Nikki explained.

"Oh yea, I guess you're right. All I remember is the captain saying they had no evidence for anything." Justin confessed.

"So anyway, as I was saying, that girl was his first victim. But I don't understand why he did it. All of a sudden, he follows this girl and kills her, why?" Nikki was perplexed at the behavior he exhibited as a teen. "And his father, there is more to that than he was willing to say. Who throws out their kid because of a single incident among teenage boys? There wasn't any fight and the police didn't even take it serious. As far as I can tell the police never even brought the missing girl suspicions anywhere. The father may not have known about her. Or maybe he knew too much!" Nikki had thought his father was holding back something ever since they spoke.

"I think we all need a good night's sleep. Let's finish our drinks and head to our rooms. Tomorrow we'll check out their finances like Justin suggested. He has to live around here somewhere. Then we'll go and talk to him. We'll see what kind of a person he is when we meet him face to face." Daniel took the last mouth full of beer from the bottle and got up from his seat. "I'll see you ladies in the morning." He walked out of the lounge without looking back.

"He is a hard man to read sometimes." Justin remarked. "I think I better turn in too, see you at breakfast."

"He didn't have much to say, did he? How do you think he feels about the case now?" Jessica wondered out loud.

"I'm not sure, but he isn't giving up on this guy as our perp. That was pretty clear." Nikki took the last sip out of her wine glass, being sure to get every drop. "I would love another one, but then I would be useless tomorrow. I'm going to head back to the room Jess, are you going to head back with me?"

"Yea, I don't think I should even finish this glass of wine. It packs a punch when you're not used to it!" Jessica said slurring her words slightly.

Once in the room Nikki used the bathroom, washed up and laid in bed. She looked over and saw that Jessica had already fallen asleep. It didn't take long before she too fell asleep.

Nikki awoke at three o'clock in the morning, and sat upright in bed. She was breathing fast and was sweating. It took her a second to realize where she was and remember what she was doing there. She went into the bathroom to get a drink of water from the faucet and splash water on her face. She stood for a minute leaning against the sink. She opened her eyes and looked into the mirror, "What is going on?" She asked herself. "It must have been the effect of the two glasses of wine." She thought to herself as she crawled back into bed and under the covers. She lay on her back with her arm across her forehead thinking of the dream she had just before she woke up.

She dreamt she was in the company of the perp, or at least that was who she thought it was. She was very much involved with whoever it was and felt extremely protective of him. She rolled onto her side. “That was not a dream that was a nightmare!” Even as she said the words to herself, the feelings she had in her dream haunted her.

~ ~ ~ ~ ~ ~ ~ ~ ~ ~ ~

“What’s wrong sweetheart?” Elizabeth asked as she woke to see her husband standing at the window in their bedroom staring outside.

“Oh, I didn’t mean to wake you.” Lobo answered without turning.

“I don’t think you did, I just woke up to use the bathroom.”

He listened as his wife got out of bed and headed down the hall. He decided that he should probably get back into bed so that she didn’t worry about him.

He woke after having another dream about someone hunting him, but this time that someone was a woman. In his dream she was everywhere he went, if he turned a corner or opened a door she was there. It was as if she was attached to him somehow. He was becoming disturbed. He rarely remembered his dreams, and when he did they had no effect on him. However the dreams that he was having lately affected him to the core of his very being. He was having feelings he had never felt before, he wasn't familiar with them and certainly didn't like them. When his wife came back to bed he reached over and pulled her toward him. He lay with his arms wrapped around her as they both fell back to sleep.

~~~~~~~~~~

Nikki woke to knocking at the door between her room and the room Daniel and Justin were in. "You awake in there?" It was Justin's voice.

"I think so, hold on a second." Jessica answered as she got up and put her robe on before answering the door.

"What's up Justin?"
~~~~~~~~~~

“When you two are up, come over here. Daniel will call down for room service, he wants to do some work on the case from here today.”

“Alright, we’ll be over shortly.”

As Jessica closed the door they could hear Justin. “Coffee is brewing ladies!”

“How did you sleep Nikki? I didn’t hear a thing once my head hit the pillow.” Jessica explained with a giggle.

“Not well. I’ve had a hard time sleeping the past couple of nights. I keep having weird dreams.”

“Really like what?” Jessica wondered.

“I don’t really remember them. I know that I’m having them though.” Nikki didn’t want to go into the details of what she remembered about the dreams. What she did remember most were the emotions she had with the dreams. She still felt them now that she was awake. They were engulfing her, strong and warm. She lay in bed a few more minutes trying to sort through what she was feeling as Jessica got her shower. She wanted to hold onto the feelings and bring them from her dream to reality. That was how good they felt within her soul. Then she thought about the man in her dream, still uncertain who he was. She didn't want to face the obvious and pushed that thought from her mind. Could there be someone out there that would be connected to her and able to fulfill her desires? She wondered.

When Jessica came out of the shower Nikki knew she had to get moving. She put the thoughts of her dream aside as she prepared for the day ahead. "Hopefully we'll make some headway today." Nikki remarked as she passed Jessica on her way into the bathroom.

"I hope so Nikki, I really hope so."

When they were both ready they headed into Daniel and Justin's room. Daniel was already busy searching data bases with his computer. Justin had papers spread across his bed, and there were more printing off the printer.

“What is all this?” Nikki asked as she poured herself a cup of coffee, and looked over the Danish pastries that were on a tray on the bureau.

“Financial records, mortgage papers, birth certificates, you name it I found it!” Daniel had a smirk on his face and a gleam in his eye.

“This half of the bed is Lobo’s paper trail, and this half is Elizabeth’s.” Justin explained.

Nikki and Jessica looked over the papers. “There’s a lot more paper work on Elizabeth’s side.” Jessica remarked.

“It seems that after they left home, everything has been in Elizabeth’s name. He doesn’t like being in the open.” Daniel explained. “His paychecks go into an account in her name by direct deposit. We found a house purchased fifteen years ago that is also in her name. But not even a car or credit card for him. Almost all we have found on him goes back to Altoona. The only thing since he left there is his job and paycheck.

“How is that possible, in this day and age to have no paper trail?” Nikki wondered out loud.

"It takes a lot of effort, and planning. He's worked hard to stay off the radar." Justin explained.

Daniel stood up and walked over to pour himself some more coffee. "I located the house that his wife owns. It's in a tiny town called Knowlton, north-east of here. It's only about twenty miles away. We could be there in an hour or less."

~~~~~~~~~~~

Elizabeth woke up to find Lobo packing his suitcase, "Are you packing for Monday?"

"I think I'm going to get an early start this time. Would you like to visit your sister for a few days? I could drop you off on my way." Lobo felt spooked, like he had to leave before his world caved in on him. He didn't want Elizabeth to sense what he believed may be coming. But he did want her safe, and out of the way.

"Sure, I'll call Loretta and tell her I'm coming." She knew not to question her husband. He had some kind of a sense that she couldn't explain, and had seen it proven accurate time and time again ever since she had known him. She went to the kitchen to
~~~~~~~~~~~

call her sister. Loretta's home was always open to her, she knew she would be welcome there, they were family. She also knew that her husband wanted her out of the way of something, something that he was running from, or avoiding.

She made arrangements for the neighbor's son to come and care for the chickens while she was gone. They lived a mile down the road, on the adjoining farm. She had hired him in the past. He was probably fourteen now, was responsible and she trusted him. He had his own flock of chickens that he would show at the yearly county fair. He won many blue ribbons over the years, which he would bring over to share with Elizabeth each year.

She went to get her bag from the back of the closet, and also packed a suitcase for her stay with Loretta.

"Loretta's looking forward to me coming and I have my bag, just in case." Elizabeth said as she packed her bags into the trunk of the car. The bag contained what she needed if she had to leave and meet him. A cell phone, cash, directions to their rendezvous spot, and a key on a piece of string.

"I have what I need too, are you set with everything?" He asked.

"Yes, I locked up and everything is turned off." She opened the car door, sat and put her seatbelt on. She looked over at her home as they pulled around to go down the driveway and wondered how long it would be before she could come back.

They drove nonstop to Loretta's home. When they arrived three screaming children came running out of the house to greet them along with a large black dog. Elizabeth and Lobo hugged their niece and nephews as they headed toward the front door. The children were very excited to see their aunt and uncle and couldn't wait for them to come into the house. Loretta stood on the porch as they approached. She hugged each one and led them into the living room.

"Is everything alright with you two?" She had a look of extreme concern on her face.

"We're fine Loretta. Lobo has business in Virginia next week and I didn't feel like staying home alone again so soon. So we decided to see if I could visit with you for a little while." Elizabeth explained.

They sat and talked for a few minutes to catch up on what was new with Loretta and the rest of the family back in Altoona. They could all feel the tension that was like an undercurrent in the room. Loretta was not relaxed, when her children came back into the room with lemonade for their aunt and uncle she found a way to get to what was waiting to burst out of her. "Charlie, why don't you take your brother, sister and Aunt Elizabeth to get her suitcase out of the car and take it to her room."

"Okay mom." The three children took Elizabeth by the hand and led her to the car to get her suitcase.

When they were out of the house Loretta turned to Lobo. "I had a phone call from an FBI agent the other day. She wanted to know where Elizabeth was and what her relationship was to you. Evidently they had been in Altoona asking questions all over town. They stopped at both your and our parents' houses. My father called me carrying on about it."

"Did they say what their names were, or why they were looking for us?"

Loretta, kept watching out the window. "All I know is that they were looking to question you about a missing woman in New York, saying that you may be a witness without realizing it. But they asked a lot of questions about that missing girl from high school and other things that went on back then. I wrote down the name of the one that called me, a Jessica Lewis. But there were four of them according to my dad, another woman and two men. Here comes Elizabeth, I don't want to upset her, you can tell her when you think it's best."

"Thank you, Loretta." He was troubled by all the information she was telling him. It was worse than he had realized.

When Elizabeth came back into the room she sensed the tension. Once she was alone with Lobo she asked him what was going on. He explained to her everything Loretta had told him. She sat on the sofa next to him holding his hand. "You better go. I'll meet you at the rendezvous spot a month from today."

"I really don't want to separate from you like this, it breaks my heart. I'm sorry." He confessed as he looked at her, she was stronger than most people realized. He gave her a kiss. "Check your phone in case I need to contact you, otherwise I'll see you in a month." He walked out the door without looking back.

Elizabeth watched as he got into the car and drove down the street and out of sight. She had no idea what would happen in the future. But for now she was going to enjoy her visit with her sister and her family.

As he drove down the street he kept rehashing what Loretta had told him. They said I might be a witness without realizing it. He knew it wasn't the truth, they had found the other women he had put in the clearing years before. They also suspected him in the disappearance of that girl in Altoona when he was in high school. He remembered her, she was the first girl he had hurt. He remembered following her, not sure of how to go about getting her alone. She was pretty, long thick brown hair and such a cute nose. Her name was Lindsey Gould, she was popular, a lot of the other girls envied her and the boys wanted to ask her out. But all he wanted to do was hurt her, which he did one Friday night. He waited near her house and when she walked by he grabbed her, it only took a second. He held her tight and slid his knife slowly into her. He could still remember the grunting sound she made and how it felt when she went limp in his arms.

~~~~~~~~~~~

The FBI agents arrived at Elizabeth's house. "It looks like no one's home, there's no car in the driveway." Justin was looking around as they drove up to the house. The driveway was long and the house stood a good distance off the road. The yard was well cared for, as was the house and small barn. The four agents walked up to the house. Daniel knocked on the door but there was no answer. After a few minutes Daniel and Jessica walked around back, and Nikki looked into the front windows. The inside was as well cared for as the outside. It was evident that the house was empty, no one was home.

"Hello, can I help you?"
~~~~~~~~~~~

Nikki and Justin turned to see a young boy riding up to the house on a bike. “Do you live here, young man?” Justin asked.

“No.” The boy turned as he saw Daniel and Jessica returning from the back of the house. The boy started to become a little nervous.

“We’re looking for Elizabeth and Lobo. Do you know where they are?” Daniel said as he and Jessica walked up to Justin and Nikki.

“They left this morning, they asked me to take care of the chickens until they get back.” The boy said.

“When will that be?” Daniel enquired.

“I don’t know, Mrs. Dylan didn’t say. Last time it was two weeks.”

“Do they go away often?” Daniel continued to question the boy.

“No, she doesn’t but he does for work. Mrs. Dylan is here most of the time.”

“Where did they go, son.” Daniel held his breath waiting for the answer.

"I don't know, she didn't say. I just want to make sure the chickens have food and water, is it alright if I do that?"

"Sure, son." Daniel was frustrated.

The team got into the van and sat watching the boy do his chores. "Do you think someone from Altoona warned them?" Daniel questioned.

"If everyone was being honest, then no. The only one who would even do that is Elizabeth's sister. But she supposedly doesn't have a phone number or address." Nikki replied, as she watched the chickens come running across the lawn to get their breakfast.

"If no one warned them, maybe the fact that they went away is a coinci…" Justin started to say coincidence but realized midsentence what was coming out of his mouth. "I mean maybe they planned a trip before he was to go to Virginia."

"Maybe, but what should we do then? Go to Virginia and wait to see if he shows up at the motel Monday?" Jessica asked. "That's six days from now. I don't think I can sit still that long on this case. Any other suggestions?"

"Why don't we check and see if we can get the EZ Pass records from today. If they used a highway maybe we'll get lucky." Justin suggested.

"It must be in the company's name, he doesn't put anything in his own name." Daniel added.

"That's a good idea. But what is our backup if they didn't use a highway, or if they did but paid the tolls with cash?" Nikki wasn't comfortable with only one avenue to go down. "I know, let's see if the house phone was used lately. I saw one on the wall when I looked into the window when you guys went around back." Nikki explained.

"That's good, Nikki." Daniel knew having Nikki on the team was a choice he wouldn't regret.

Daniel started the engine and slowly drove down the driveway. He was glad that they had a direction to go in, hopefully one of them would give them a lead to pursue. If they didn't he knew that they would just be grabbing at straws from here on out.

They arrived back at the hotel about forty-five minutes later. On the way Daniel divvied out a few tasks for them to do once they arrived.

Once back in their room, Daniel contacted the Oak Tree Land Development Corporation to see what motel they booked for Lobo in Virginia. He also checked the EZ Pass site and found that the corporation did have EZ Passes, ten of them to be exact. He checked the online data base for activity. Their employees had used their passes in the Philadelphia area, New Jersey, and Massachusetts. There wasn't anything in the part of Pennsylvania were they were looking. The good news was that he was given the name of the motel in Staunton, Virginia. The Midlantic Inn.

Nikki checked the phone records. They were in Elizabeth's name, no surprise there. There were no calls into the home for at least a month. But there was one out, that morning at seven minutes after nine to Dunkansville. The call lasted about three minutes. They couldn't have had much of a conversation in that amount of time, Nikki thought.

Jessica checked travel agencies and airlines with no results.

Justin checked credit card transactions with no results for Elizabeth. It seemed there were no credit cards in either one of their names.

The four shared their information and decided to go to Dunkansville and see if Lobo and Elizabeth where there. Or if Elizabeth's sister Loretta had any new information.

They left Wilkes-Barre at one-thirty and arrived at Loretta's house at three-forty five. Daniel parked across the street and down a couple houses. They sat and watched the house for a little while.

"I don't see a car there. Not even one for Loretta's husband, he must be at work." Jessica pointed out.

"I suppose we should go knock on the door and see what Loretta knows." Daniel opened his door and the other three followed him across the street.

Once at the door Daniel knocked. They heard a large dog bark, and the sound of children coming toward the door. The door opened revealing a young boy about ten years old. "Hello, is your mother or father home?" Daniel asked.

"Yea. Mom, it's for you." The boy called.

A few seconds later a woman in her late twenties came to the door. She was slim, light brown hair and brown eyes. "Can I help you?"

"Good morning, are you Loretta, Elizabeth Dylan's sister?" Daniel asked.

"Yes."

"Do you know where she or her husband might be?"

"She's here with me, visiting." Loretta almost told them she had no idea, but didn't want to start something she felt she would not be able to deal with if they found out differently.

"Can I speak with her?" Daniel tried to remain unmoved, but inside he had a welling of excitement.

"Hold on, let me see if she's up. She was tired and laid down earlier." Loretta left the agents on the porch while she went to speak with her sister. She knocked on the bedroom door. "Lizzy, Lizzy, are you awake?"

"I'm just resting, come in." Elizabeth answered.

Loretta opened the door. "There are four people here asking for you, it must be those FBI agents." Loretta's voice revealed her fear for her sister.

"Really, why would they be looking for me? I'll be right down." Elizabeth took a deep breath. Lobo had prepared her for the day she might have to deal with a situation like this.

Loretta went downstairs and let the agents into the house. "She'll be right down, have a seat in the living room. Can I get you anything to drink?"

Daniel answered for them all. "No thank you, we'll only be here a few minutes."

The four sat silent. A few minutes later Elizabeth walked down the stairs. She was thin, about five foot three with light brown hair. She had a slight limp, as she walked across the living room and sat down in a chair. “What can I do for you?” She asked.

“Hello Mrs. Dylan, my name is Daniel these are my partners, Justin, Jessica and Nikki. We wanted to speak with your husband, is he around?” Daniel asked.

“No, he left for business this morning.” Elizabeth was to the point and quick to answer only what they asked, adding nothing. Just as she had been coached to do.

“We have a couple of questions for him. Do you know where we can contact him?” Daniel continued.

“He is heading to Virginia, I don’t know exactly where. He usually calls me once he gets there. Can I ask what this is about?” Elizabeth wanted to find out what they had to say so she could relay the information to her husband.

“Sure, we think he may have witnessed an abduction in New York. He could be an important witness without realizing it. Do you have his cell number?” Daniel waited to hear her answer. So far she seemed to be oblivious to why they would be looking for her husband.

"Yes, I'll write it down for you." She walked over to her purse and took out a pen and small notebook. She wrote in the notebook and then ripped out the piece of paper and handed it to Daniel.

"Thank you Mrs. Dylan." Daniel said as he and the rest of the team stood up to leave.

"Do you have a lot of problems with your injury? I don't mean to pry but we had been told you were in an accident with your family in Altoona." Nikki watched to see what her reaction would be.

"Sometimes. It really depends on the weather, or if I overdo it. How is my family, I don't really keep in touch with them, only Loretta." Elizabeth was curious to what her answer would be.

"We didn't see your mom but your dad seemed alright." Nikki was surprised that she continued the conversation without hesitation.

When the small talk was over, the four agents made their way to the door to leave. Elizabeth watched as they walked across the street to their van. She was glad they were on their way. Loretta came up behind her. “Are you okay?”

“Yes. But I don’t really understand why they are so persistent. If Lobo is a witness to something that he might not even know about, it really doesn’t make sense. Didn’t you say earlier that the one who called you was named Jessica?”

“Yea, was she one of them? I tried to listen but it was hard from the kitchen.” Loretta confessed.

“She was, but she didn’t say anything. Only the one guy named Daniel and the younger woman named Nikki. I think she was trying to make me nervous, she made sure I knew they had spoken to dad back in Altoona.” Elizabeth closed the door once the van started to drive away.

“I don’t like it Lizzy, do you think they will be hanging around here or keep coming back?”

“I hope not. I planned on leaving in a few weeks, but maybe I should leave sooner. If they come back again I will. I don’t want to cause you any problems Loretta.”

“I don’t care about them coming back here. I don’t want you to get upset.” Loretta was worried for her sister.

“Charles will mind, he doesn’t really care for Lobo as it is. I’m not really comfortable just sitting here waiting to see if they come back. If they think Lobo will be back here they will hang around and come back, don’t you think? If I’m gone they will have no reason to come here.” Elizabeth was uneasy with this whole situation and wanted to go where she would be away from it.

“Alright Lizzy, but I’m going to drive you wherever you want to go. You aren’t just getting on a bus or something.”

“Sure, Loretta, you can drive me. Let me think about it.” The sisters hugged.

Elizabeth went back to her room, took out the disposable cell and sent a text to Lobo. She relayed to him the names and descriptions of the agents as well as the van's color. She also texted him of her conversation with them.

They had been prepared for this. The phone number that she gave the agents was another phone that had a recorded message stating that Mr. Dylan was unable to answer right now, but would get back to whoever was calling as soon as he was able. Then asked for a message.

~ ~ ~ ~ ~ ~ ~ ~ ~ ~ ~

Once in the van Daniel dialed the phone number Elizabeth gave him. "It goes to a recorded message." He remarked to the team. "He either has no signal or doesn't answer while driving."

"Maybe he screens his calls!" Nikki remarked.

"This is Daniel Dillon, I work for the FBI and needed to ask you a question concerning your time recently in New York State. Please give me a call at this number." Daniel left his phone number and hung up. "I doubt he'll call back, but then again one never knows."

"Do you think he really left the area? Could she be lying for him?" Jessica wondered.

"She is either being honest, or has rehearsed this because she seemed genuine to me." Nikki gave her opinion. "She seemed a little too calm. She answered what we asked but really didn't have much of a reaction either way. Not even when I mentioned we had been in Altoona. She covered for him when they were teenagers and would probably do it now. What do you guys think?"

"She did seem a little rehearsed, now that you mention it Nikki. I'm sure her sister told her of the conversation I had with her. Someone from Altoona may have called Loretta and she in turn would have told Elizabeth." Jessica remarked.

"That is a possibility." Nikki conceded.

"I don't believe he's around here. I think he dropped her off at her sister's because he thought we might come looking for him. Where he is however is another matter. I really doubt he went to Virginia, but we'll have to check it out." Daniel stated as he started the van and headed toward the center of town to get them all dinner. They hadn't eaten since breakfast.

CHAPTER ELEVEN

After leaving Elizabeth at Loretta's home, Lobo drove east. He was going to wait for Elizabeth at the rendezvous spot they had spoken of many times. He knew that his whole life was spent in a country setting, including the dark things he had done. Because of this they had decided to hide out in a place that was totally the opposite.

As he drove closer the traffic became more congested, he wasn't used to driving bumper to bumper. He began to wonder if he would be able to tolerate living in a city. He made his way down the one way streets until he came to 34th Street where he turned and drove till he came to Sansom Street. He made a left turn and found a parking space. He sat for a moment, looked around at the neighborhood, and then got out of the car. As he stood on the sidewalk people were walking all around him. The traffic noises were constant, horns were beeping, engines gunning, and the occasional tire squealed. He could smell the exhaust from the traffic as he looked for the address he had memorized almost a year ago. When he arrived at the doorway, he saw that it was next to an Irish Pub. There were tables and chairs on the sidewalk in front, with black metal fencing about three feet tall surrounding them. He pulled the key from his pocket, unlocked the door, reached over and turned the doorknob. As the door opened he peered inside and down a dark hallway that had a sunlit room at the end. He searched the wall for a light switch, it was on the left side. He turned the light on to see clearly to the room at the far end of the hallway, about ten feet away. As he walked toward the room he noticed how bright it appeared. Once in the room he looked out the window that was on the far side of the room. It faced out the back of the building into a yard that had bushes surrounded by a wooden fence about six feet tall, a small grassy plot was inside the bushes. The living room was nice, it had a tan rug, colonial type furniture with end tables, a television and a reclining chair. On the far right was a doorway, he walked through into a kitchen furnished with a table and chairs. Off to the right were two doorways, the first led to a bedroom that was also fully furnished. The second led to a bathroom that had a frilly shower curtain. As he relaxed in the reclining chair he found it amazing how quiet it was in the apartment. The sounds from outside couldn't be heard unless they were extremely loud.

He had found this apartment a little over a year ago in an ad in the Philadelphia Press and had been paying rent ever since.

He went into the bedroom and began to unpack and settle into what would be his home. When he took out his disposable cell he noticed that the light was flashing. He pushed on the button to read the text, it was from Elizabeth.

He sat on the bed reading her text over a couple of times to remember the details. When he read one of the names a chill ran down his spine, as the woman in his dream flashed into his thoughts. Could this person be her, could Nikki be the one haunting him in his sleep?

He texted Elizabeth back, acknowledging that he got her text and that he was safe.

~~~~~~~~~~
~~~~~~~~~~

Daniel pulled up to the motel in Wilkes-Barre at nine that night. On the way home they rehashed all the information they had, and what avenues where now open to them. They decided that they would split up. Justin and Daniel would go to Virginia to see if he was going to show up there. Jessica and Nikki would stay in Wilkes-Barre to follow up on any new leads that came along.

~ ~ ~ ~ ~ ~ ~ ~ ~ ~ ~

Lobo awoke early the next morning. He had slept well without any dreams. He showered, dressed, and went to find a cup of coffee and some breakfast. He stopped at a small restaurant on 34th street. Then a corner grocery store to purchase a few groceries before heading home. He spent the day watching television, and took another walk in the evening. He stopped by the Irish Pub for a drink, talked to a couple of the locals, and then went home to retire for the night.

The next couple days were repeats of the day before. He knew that this wasn't going to be tolerable for any length of time. He took out his computer and searched for a road map to Atlantic City. He wanted to get away for a couple of days to break up the monotony. He was glad to see that it was almost a straight line from Philadelphia to the shore.

He took a few minutes and looked at what the area around his destination was like. There was a large forest not far away, he would have to go north on the Parkway to reach it. Maybe a day trip to check it out would be nice to do the following weekend. But for now it was Saturday and he felt a visit to a casino might be just the thing.

He drove across the Benjamin Franklin Bridge, and then headed down the Atlantic City Expressway. He made sure he paid cash for the tolls to avoid detection. When he arrived he parked in the parking garage next to the Carousel Casino and Hotel. As he entered the casino he had hopes to relax and maybe win a few dollars.

He walked around feeling a little overwhelmed by all the activity within the casino until he came to the slot machines. He took a seat and began pushing the buttons on the Texas Hold'em slot machine. Time passed quickly, he found it easy to play the odds and double his money. Playing against a computer and not a person was comforting to him. Computers play the odds rather than making decisions based on emotion. He felt this gave him an edge since he too looked at things by comparing the odds.

He left the casino at two in the morning with a profit of a hundred and twenty dollars. On his way back to his car he noticed someone leaning up against one of the cement pillars in the parking garage. He had to pass her to get to his car. "Are you alright Miss?" He asked.

The girl slowly turned, she was obviously drunk. "Can you take me out of here? I can't seem to find my friends or our car?"

"Where do you want to go?" He asked as he looked around to see if anyone else was around, and then to see if there were any cameras.

"I don't care." She answered as she approached Lobo barely able to walk straight.

He helped her into the car, before getting in himself. As he left the garage he made sure no one saw them. He looked over at the young woman, she was a strawberry blonde, thin but not skinny, she was his type. He drove out of Atlantic City, turned right down Route 9 and across the Mullica River and north on the Parkway. The Pine Barrens reminded him of parts of New York, only the land was flat, not mountainous. The sun was coming up as he drove down a dirt road made for firefighters. He stopped the car and reached under his seat, attached to the underside of the car seat was his knife. He slid the knife out of the rawhide holster he kept it in and then from under the seat. He got out of the car and went around to the passenger side door, he opened the door and awoke the young woman. "Wake up, can you hear me, wake up!" He said as he gently nudged her shoulder.

She opened her eyes and rubbed her face, then rubbed her eyes with her hands. "Where am I?"

"You were pretty wasted, and asked me to give you a lift from the casino. Do you remember?"

"Not really." She pulled her legs to the side of the car seat and stood up outside of the car. "Where are we?"

"I wanted to make sure you were alright before I took you home." He reached over for her hand. "Let's take a walk to sober you up the rest of the way." He led her down the dirt road a few hundred feet, before pulling her toward him.

She startled at his sudden shift in demeanor.

He looked into her eyes, at first there was fear, then as she realized he wasn't going to rape her, she relaxed.

"You scared me for a second there." She said as she leaned into him and turned her head upward to kiss him.

He pulled her toward him as if to hug her, as he did he brought up his knife between them and slid it into her right upper abdomen. She gasped and let out a guttural sound at the same time. She attempted to push away from him, but he was stronger, he pulled his knife out of her and pulled her as close to him as possible. Holding her tight with his left arm as she struggled to get away he focused on every movement and sound she made. He smelled the sweet perfume that was in her hair as he brought his right hand around her and pushed his knife into the left side of her mid back. She gasped and squealed. He felt her shudder in pain. Instead of fighting she leaned more into him, this was his favorite part, she was succumbing to him. He pulled the knife from her, hugged her tight with both his arms relishing the moment. His senses were totally engulfed in feeling her every movement and sound. She was whimpering and then she started to gasp for breathe. He then pushed the knife into the right side of her mid back. He felt her knees buckle as he held her tight, then her head slumped backward. He looked at her still, silent face, tranquil and so young.

He picked her up and carried her into the trees far enough from the dirt road so no one would easily see her. He returned to his car opened the trunk and took out a plastic garbage bag. He put his knife and bloody shirt into the bag. He then opened the hatch that housed the spare tire and pulled out another bag, replacing it with the bag of his bloody clothing. Inside there was a fresh shirt and other assorted clothing. He put a fresh shirt on and went to sit in his car.

He needed that; the stress of this past week had been building up inside him. Releasing it made him feel like a new man. He made a K turn and drove out of the Pine Barrens. He arrived back at his home in Philadelphia at seven in the morning and went to bed.

When he woke up at ten-thirty he made a fresh pot of coffee. After drinking a cup he went to his car where he removed the black plastic garbage bag. He then sprayed the passenger seat, dashboard, and the door inside and out with window cleaner using paper towels to wipe any residue that the young woman may have left. Once back in his apartment he removed his clothes from the bag to wash them and to rinse his knife off. That night he placed his knife back under the car seat where it belonged and replaced the bags as they had been with a fresh shirt.

~ ~ ~ ~ ~ ~ ~ ~ ~ ~ ~

The morning after visiting with Elizabeth in Duncansville, the team met over coffee in the hotel restaurant. They discussed their plan for the next few days. As decided the night before, Daniel and Justin would drive down to Virginia while Jessica and Nikki would continue to do research and look for new leads.

After returning to their room, Nikki continued to search the data banks of the FBI and state police in the surrounding states. She focused on Virginia first around Craigsville and Staunton.

Jessica was busy logging everyone they had spoken with and their connection to their suspect into their journal.

"Come here and look at this." Nikki had found something.

"What is it?" Jessica was curious, and hoped it was a lead.

"A year ago, and two years ago, women went missing in Virginia. The first from Goshen, and the second from Raphine. Both are in close proximity to Staunton. Get this they were in their late twenties, one had brown hair was five feet four and weighed one hundred and twenty five pounds. The other was a blonde, five foot five and a hundred and twenty pounds. If these women are his victims they would fit because all his victims are very similar yet different. He doesn't have a specific type, like all blondes, but all are similar. Like if a guy was dating and found slightly different types of women attractive." Nikki hesitated as she thought about what to say next.

"This guy isn't picking victims that are reminders of someone in his past. He chooses them by what he finds attractive about them. But instead of looking for a date, he looks for a victim. I think he seduces them into feeling safe with him before he kills them. That would explain why no one has ever noticed when he took them. If the victims felt they were in danger, if they were afraid at all, someone would have picked up on that. But they may not notice two people who are not acting any different than you come across every day. No one really pays much attention to that."

"So what you're saying then Nikki, is that he is replacing a sexual experience with the act of killing."

"Yes. I think that's what I'm saying. Do you think that makes sense?" Nikki looked to Jessica who had more experience with profiles.

"Yes, it does. Actually it does." Jessica went over and picked up the pictures of all the victims, looking at them in a different light.

“His first victim that we suspect was Lindsey Gould she was sixteen years old, he was fifteen. As he ages his victims get older, also. Mellany Short was twenty-six and he was thirty-one. Then for some reason he goes after Suzy Malloy who was only twenty-two while he is thirty-four.”

“Maybe he’s having a midlife crises?” Nikki realized her joke was in poor taste. “Sorry about that, it really isn’t funny.”

“You might have a point though, Nikki. He may have found Suzy attractive, as an older man might find a pretty young girl. But unlike other men who would not pursue her due to their age difference. He however, would most likely not have that social stigma to stop him.”

“Maybe we should call Daniel and tell him about the two missing women, they should be getting close to Virginia by now.” Nikki suggested.

“Yea, we should. Why don’t you call since you found the information? I’ll finish organizing these notes, I’m almost done.”

Jessica said as she walked back over to the papers spread out over the bed.

Justin answered the phone and Nikki gave him the names and places that the women went missing from. They decided to stay in Virginia long enough to check out the circumstances that surrounded the cases. First stop however, was the Midlantic Inn located in Staunton. They would get a room there and wait to see if Lobo showed up.

An hour later when Daniel and Justin reached the motel they registered and then asked if their friend had arrived yet.

The desk clerk checked the computer. “I’m afraid he cancelled, looks like it was yesterday late in the morning.” He saw the look on Daniel’s face as he told him the news. “I’m sorry.”

“Something must have come up suddenly. We’ll still be staying a few days. We have some business to take care of.” Daniel replied as he took the key card from the clerk that would open the door to their room.

Once they settled into the room, Daniel called Jessica and relayed the news to her and Nikki of Lobo's cancelling of the room in Virginia. He also told her that he and Justin where going to check out the information on the missing women and would head back Friday. If that changed he would call.

They spent the rest of the day planning their route to Goshen and Raphine. They would drive south to Raphine, then west to Goshen. They also thought it would be of interest to head north and check out Craigsville. The area where the Land Development Cooperation was interested in purchasing property. Then they would head northeast back to Staunton.

After hanging up the phone Jessica looked at Nikki. "If Lobo is not going to Virginia, then where is he?"

"If I were him I would be looking to disappear. He knows we're looking for him, I think he left town to hide out." Nikki thought for a moment. "I bet Elizabeth will be joining him. We should put a tail on her."

Jessica agreed and made the necessary phone calls.

That night Nikki dreamt that she was looking for someone, searching dark rooms that after she entered there was no way out. Somehow though she would end up in another room. She dreamt that while she was in one of the rooms a shadow came from behind her and engulfed her. She wasn't afraid of the shadow, she felt warm as though the shadow was familiar. She knew it was Lobo, or a symbol of him. As it engulfed her, she felt as though the shadow had some kind of control over her. She tried to go to another room but the shadow pulled at her. She was frustrated and struggled against the darkness around her without success, then…

"Nikki, Nikki, wake up!" She heard Jessica's voice.

It took her a second to focus. "What's wrong Jess?"

"You must have been dreaming, you where mumbling and tossing around in bed." Jessica explained.

"Oh, yea. I think I was. I remember now. It was weird. It really didn't make any sense. What time is it?"

Jessica looked at the clock on the table. "Three-forty."

"We better get back to sleep." Nikki didn't want to talk about it anymore.

"Okay, I'll see you in the morning." Jessica crawled back into bed and quickly fell back to sleep.

Nikki had trouble getting back to sleep. The dream she had was different but the feelings in the dream where the same. She felt very strongly for the entity in the dream, she welcomed it surrounding her the way it had. It was difficult to pull away and wake up. To separate herself from it. The dream haunted her just as the others she had recently did. She knew that they were more than dreams; there was a connection to this case, to Lobo.

She turned to her other side out of reflex. The thought of having positive feelings toward the man who killed Stacey was too much for her to deal with, even if it was a dream.

~~~~~~~~~~

Nikki and Jessica spent Thursday searching for other possible victims. They discussed the time frames of the women who were definitely victims, along with the possible ones. "If he killed
~~~~~~~~~~

Lindsey Gould in 1994, the next victim wasn't for ten years in Wilkes-Barre." Nikki pointed out.

"Let's look at those years and see where he was." Jessica suggested.

"Well, we know that he was in Altoona till he was eighteen. There is no record of anyone going missing or anything else during that time. Then he leaves when he is eighteen with Elizabeth. Maybe she was enough for him until he saw Nancy Walnick. He's attracted to her, so he kills her to fulfill his desire. She would have been the start, a year later is when he took Stacey. Then there is a five year gap, or at least a five year span of time with no victims that we know of. Then if we include the two Virginia women that are missing, there's a victim every year for four years. If we don't count them then we have another three year gap between Mellany Short and Suzy Lamoy." Nikki stopped to think.

"Or, we just haven't found who else is missing. All we know for sure is that no one was listed as a murder victim within those gaps. Missing persons don't show up as readily." Jessica added.

"Let's take a break. I'm starving and my brain is starting to hurt from too much thinking." Nikki said as she got up from her computer to stretch.

"Good idea, we can come back fresh after." Jessica agreed as she started to put her shoes on.

After lunch Daniel called to catch Jessica and Nikki up on what he and Justin had found. "We had one development, the woman from Raphine disappeared without a trace. However the woman from Goshen was seen with a man by a paperboy delivering newspapers after school. The boy said that he recognized her because she was one of the paper's customers and was on his route. He saw her at a drug store, she was waiting outside when a man walked over to her. They spoke and she walked with him around the corner and down the street. The boy didn't follow, there didn't seem to be anything wrong. He did say that whoever the man was, he wasn't local, but he was well dressed and had black hair. Who does that sound like?"

“That’s our best lead so far connecting our perp. Did the local police have anything to say about their investigation?” Jessica asked.

“They tried to find the man but it was a dead end.” Daniel added.

“We made a little headway, we’ll tell you about it when you get back. We also had a tail placed on Elizabeth.”

“Good idea Jessica. We’re going to start heading back this evening. When we get tired we’ll get a motel room. We’ll see you two tomorrow. Bye for now”

“Bye.” Jessica turned to Nikki. “I think we can add the Virginia women to our list.”

CHAPTER TWELVE

Daniel and Justin arrived back in Wilkes-Barre at one o'clock in the afternoon. They settled into their room and then invited Jessica and Nikki over to discuss what they had found.

Nikki showed the timeline she and Jessica made of the victims, and their ages as compared to the perps. She then explained her theory that she and Jessica had talked about. That he was replacing a sexual act with the act of murder.

Daniel and Justin were intrigued. "That's very good, Nikki." Justin stated.

"It explains a lot. Like why the women's descriptions aren't quite the same." Daniel added.

"I had a tap put on Elizabeth's cell and the phone at Loretta's house. If he and Elizabeth are communicating it isn't on either one of those phones." Daniel was perplexed at the dead ends that they kept coming up against and it showed in his voice each time he talked about one of them.

"He's using a burner phone! Remember the call to Suzy, it was traced back to an untraceable phone. He must use them all the time. He and Elizabeth must be talking with a phone that can't be traced." Nikki exclaimed.

"How can we find that out?" Jessica asked. "Is it possible?"

"I don't think we can unless we know the place he bought them, and the carrier of the service." Justin added.

"Yea, the technology isn't that good yet. It's another dead end I'm afraid." Daniel said in a low monotone voice. He was losing hope of catching Lobo. He seemed to always be a step ahead of them. Daniel knew he had planned for this day way in advance.

Nikki was concerned about Daniel's defeated attitude in this case and decided to ask him what was going on. He had been so different when it started. "Can I talk to you in private?" She asked when the other two were occupied and didn't notice.

"Sure Nikki, let's take a walk to the ice machine. I have some soda that's warm and I don't like to drink it that way."

“Hey, we’ll be right back. We’re going to get some ice.” Daniel said as he grabbed the ice bucket off the table.

Once in the hall and away from the door Nikki stopped. Daniel did the same. “I’m worried about you Daniel. You seem like you’re losing hope of catching this guy.”

Daniel looked at Nikki for a second, he hadn’t realized it showed. “I’m sorry Nikki. I usually find it so easy to catch the perps I go after. This guy is different, he’s in control. His urges don’t have more control over him. He has enough control over them to function. He’s smart, and intuitive. He’s planned for the day we would start looking for him. He knew it would happen. He doesn’t think he is above being caught, and wants to be sure he isn’t.”

Nikki listened intently to every word Daniel said.

“That’s why I wanted you on this team, Nikki, you’re intuitive. I don’t think we can catch him without you. I feel inferior to him at times. I’m sorry that it shows.”

“I don’t know what to say!” Nikki was embarrassed.

“You don’t have to say anything. Let’s just go get some ice before they start looking for us.” He laughed as he started down the hallway.

When they returned to the room the mood was lighter. Justin had taken the soda out of the bag and was preparing to pour some in a cup, while Jessica was flipping the TV channels looking for something to watch. They relaxed the rest of the night watching television, eating chips and drinking soda.

Saturday was uneventful. When they met for breakfast Sunday morning they decided to eat away from the motel. They were getting a little tired of the same menu every day. There was a Pancake Restaurant a couple miles down the road. They had seen the commercial on TV the day before and thought that filled French toast sounded pretty good.

The restaurant had televisions hanging around for the customers to look at while eating. Some had cartoons for the children, the one above them had a twenty four hour news station on.

While they were waiting for the waitress to bring the check Justin pointed up at the screen. “Look, what is that about?” Scrolling along the bottom was a news flash of a missing woman from Atlantic City.

They all stood reading the scroll. Daniel went to the cash register to get the check himself and paid for their meal. Returning to the table he announced, “Let’s go find out what the story is about.”

Once in the van Daniel called the police in Atlantic City for the details. From the conversation the rest of the team had a pretty good idea of what had happened. When Daniel hung up he turned in his seat. “We’re going to Atlantic City.” He filled them in on the details of the missing woman as they drove back to the motel to pack up and then head to New Jersey.

They arrived in New Jersey at two fifteen that afternoon and went right to the Atlantic City Police Station. Daniel introduced himself and his team to the Chief of Detectives, Milton Richmond. “I’m glad you’re here, I called the casino and they’re expecting us.”

They followed the detective's car through the narrow side streets, and across the main highway that ran through Atlantic City to the Houseboat Hotel and Casino. When they arrived there was a news crew waiting at the entrance to the casino. As the team walked up to them a man with a microphone came over. "Are you really from the FBI? Why would a missing woman have the FBI involved in the case so quickly?" The reporter was relentless as the team pushed passed him and the camera to enter the casino.

A security guard met them inside and took them to a room down a hall by the cashier windows. "I looked at the camera footage from all the elevators, exits and entrances. According to the woman's friends she left the Houseboat close to two in the morning. She had too much to drink and was going to go sit in the car. When they arrived, not too long after, they couldn't find her. She didn't return home and isn't answering her phone."

"Here we go. See there." The security guard pointed at the video. "She's in the elevator here. You can tell she's in no condition to be alone, she keeps stumbling around. The next camera to pick her up is the one to the south side of the lot. We share our parking garage with the Carousel Casino, she wandered over to their section of the garage so she never made it to the car she came in."

"Do you have any footage of that side of the lot?" Daniel asked.

"We have to go over to their security office, they know we're coming. This is bad publicity for us. We are certainly worried about the poor woman but are also concerned for business. The last thing we need is a serial killer running around Atlantic City."

They walked across the enclosed bridge that attached the two casinos. When they came to the security office the chief of security was just as forthcoming. He showed them his video. "We found the woman entering our part of the garage here, she stumbled out into the lot and out of site of the camera. But the interesting thing is that there was only one car that left the lot between one-thirty and four that morning." He pulled up another feed on a different screen. "Right here, there is a dark colored SUV, you can see two people in the front. The one in the passenger seat is lying up against the window, which could be her."

"Is there a better view?" Justin asked.

"Not from our cameras." The security chief answered.

"I have something." The detective stated. "We have cameras on the traffic lights to catch speeders and the taxi's that run red lights. It's a big problem and has caused a lot of accidents. Anyway I have this from the camera at the light that leads to the White Horse Pike." The detective pulled a cassette out of his pocket and gave it to the security chief, who put the cassette into the video player attached to the monitor.

At a certain place in the video the detective pushed the pause button. "There, we believe that's her in the passenger seat."

The four FBI agents looked at the picture. It was fuzzy but was definitely him. "That's him driving, there's no doubt about it." Daniel couldn't believe his eyes. "Can we have a copy of that?"

"You can have that one, I made it for you." The detective handed it to Daniel after ejecting it from the video player.

"Where does the White Horse Pike lead to?" Justin asked.

"It heads west out of the city to Absecon. From there he could have gone anywhere." The detective explained.

"Is there a forest nearby, or a large wooded area?" Daniel asked.

"There are a lot of wooded areas, and the Pine Barrens are just north of here. Why do you ask?" The detective wondered.

"Our suspect has taken the bodies of the women he murdered and placed them in wooded areas so that they are hidden from site." Daniel explained. "We aren't sure how familiar he is with the area, but I don't think he would drive far with her. I would say that wherever he took her it was within an hour radius of here."

"The state troopers patrol most of the areas where he would have gone. I'll contact them and let them know you are here, I just need contact information." The fact that the detective wanted this taken care of as soon as possible was very evident.

"We haven't found a motel yet, but I will give you our cell numbers." Daniel wrote the four numbers down for the detective who in turn gave them his personal number.

"I would suggest that you stay at either the Highroller Inn, it's outside the city on the Pike heading west, or the Morris Hotel. The Morris is farther inland near the Parkway entrance. They'll both give you a discount since you are here as law enforcement." The detective added.

"Thank you, we'll be at one of them." They shook hands and left the casino to find a motel.

~ ~ ~ ~ ~ ~ ~ ~ ~ ~ ~

Lobo was sitting watching the news and playing solitaire when a news report came on about the missing woman in Atlantic City. He watched intently to see what they knew.. He was relieved to see that they had not found her, and had no idea what happened. The news castor flashed footage of the FBI agents who came to investigate the disappearance. He felt a cold chill in his stomach, this wasn't good. He then saw the four agents as they headed into the casino. He looked closely at the two women, then at one in particular. "It's her!" He said out loud. He picked up the controller to the cable box and replayed the footage. He paused the picture at the point where he could see the woman clearest. Without a doubt, he knew, this was the woman from his dreams, this was Nikki. She was the key, before her he had always been invisible. Now he felt like he was in the open, he was being unmasked. She had to go, if he was going to disappear and not be on their radar any longer, she definitely had to go.

He began to set his sights on Nikki, the hunt was on. He would stalk her, separate her from the others, and kill her. If it was the last thing he would ever do. He knew that he had no choice. She would be his downfall otherwise.

He took out his phone and sent Elizabeth a text. "Roost." She would know exactly what he meant.

~ ~ ~ ~ ~ ~ ~ ~ ~ ~ ~

Monday evening Elizabeth checked her phone and saw Lobo's message. She smiled, then went downstairs to see her sister. "Loretta, I think I'll go back home. Can you still take me or should I get a bus ticket?"

"I'll take you, are you sure you want to go back so soon, we hardly see each other anymore."

"Why don't you and the kids take me on Friday and then stay for the weekend, we can go into town for lunch." Elizabeth suggested.

"Will Lobo be meeting us? Charles might want to come if he thinks Lobo will be there."

"No, he won't be there. I'm not sure when he'll be back." Elizabeth really didn't want Charles to come. He tolerated her but made it quite clear that he didn't like her husband.

Charles came in the door and overheard the last part of their conversation. Loretta realized this. "I was going to take Elizabeth home on Friday and spend the weekend there. Do you want to come?"

"I would love too, but I have that golf tournament this weekend at work. We're raising money for a local charity to send disabled children to camp this summer."

"Oh yea, I remember you mentioning that. I just didn't realize that it was this coming weekend. It works out well then since you weren't going to be home anyway." Loretta was relieved, she loved her husband, and they normally had a very good relationship, their only problem was Elizabeth's marriage. Charles felt Lobo had some kind of problem from the first day he met him. He didn't like his wife or children alone with the man.

That night when Loretta and Charles where alone in bed Charles brought up the subject. "If Lobo does show up, I want you and the kids to come home early. Do you understand?"

"Yes, I do hun. But Lobo is fine. I know that I tell you this all the time and you don't believe it. He would never hurt me or the kids. Where did that even come from with you?"

"I'm not going to fight with you about this, you have always respected my feelings and I appreciate that. I love you and the kids. I just don't trust Lobo. I was there in 1994 when Lindsey Gould disappeared. Lobo had something to do with that, I know he did. Lindsey hung out with the guys on the football team. You know that, she was a cheerleader and liked Mike. I was there the night she had a little too much to drink and started talking about how Lobo was following her around. A week later she was missing. I knew her well enough to know that she wasn't prone to making things up, or getting over excited. I believed that he was following her. I told that to the police. But your sister said Lobo was with her during the time Lindsey disappeared. They never even questioned him that I know of, not officially anyway."

"Elizabeth says he won't be there, so as long as he isn't there then we'll stay. I promise."

"Thank you." Charles said as he leaned over and kissed his wife goodnight.

~~~~~~~~~~~

Daniel and the rest of their team checked into the Highroller Inn. Their rooms were on the sixth floor with a nice view of the area surrounding the motel. The view was mostly marshland, the bay was beyond with a boat or two anchored in the water while the occupants fished. Atlantic City could be seen in the background
~~~~~~~~~~~

with a windmill farm sprouting up from the bay in front of the skyline of the city. They were unable to get adjoining rooms, but they were able to get rooms on the same floor. However they were at opposite ends of the hall. Daniel was uncomfortable with the set up. But since there was a conference in town for the upcoming weekend, most of the rooms in the hotels and motels were booked.

“There would be an International Conference here this weekend.” Daniel remarked as they stepped out of the elevator and each pair walked toward their rooms.

Once in their room, Nikki and Jessica unpacked and settled in for the night. While lying in their beds they talked about the case, and what they thought would be their next move.

“Do you think he’s in Atlantic City?” Nikki asked. “It really doesn’t fit his profile to be in a populated place like this.”

“I don’t know, Nikki. But that was definitely him in the car. He could be anywhere, I suppose. He could have even returned to Pennsylvania!” Jessica answered.

"We could be running around in circles chasing him if we don't watch it." Nikki remarked as she turned the light out by her bed and pulled the covers up to her head.

When Daniel and Justin got to their room, Justin noticed that Daniel was in a foul mood. He wondered what happened between the van and now to cause it. "Are you okay Daniel, you seem out of sorts."

"I'm worried that's all. It's taking so long to pin this guy down. I just hope we don't lose him. Right now I'm not sure even where to go next with this case. Any suggestions?" Daniel hated feeling helpless and that was the feeling he was beginning to have with this case.

"I just keep looking to see where the next sign will come from, like that news report that led us here. He knows we're after him. He's slipping up, making mistakes. I don't believe that the woman he took at the casino was planned. She was a crime of opportunity. So he didn't prepare, and that showed with the pictures we got from the cameras."

“You have a good point, Justin, she probably was. So why was he here then?” Daniel wondered.

“Maybe he was on a vacation. He could have come here to gamble or take in a show? Who knows, but it wasn’t to kill that woman. It just ended up that way.”

“Let’s sleep on that. When we’re fresh in the morning we’ll see where it takes us.” Daniel yawned and walked over to his bed.

They put the television on to watch the news. They saw the pictures of themselves at the casino and the newscaster’s voice stating they were there to find the missing woman. They flashed a picture of the young woman on the screen with her name and description. Daniel lay watching, wondering how many more women would be murdered before they would get him.

Tuesday through Thursday came and went. Daniel, Justin, Nikki, and Jessica kept in touch with the local police and state troopers with no further developments. They tried to get the license plate of the car Lobo drove enlarged to read it, but the angle of the photograph made it impossible.

No one heard from or found the body of the missing woman. The local police, firemen and volunteers searched the forest and wooded areas within a fifty mile radius of Atlantic City without any sign of her.

On Friday while the team met to decide where, if anyplace they would go from here, Daniel's phone rang. "Hello… yes this is he." Daniel listened for a few minutes. "Alright keep me posted."

"It seems that Loretta drove Elizabeth back to her home this morning." Daniel seemed defeated. "I suppose she isn't going to meet him anywhere after all."

"Is he going to head back there?" Jessica wondered.

"He knows we're after him. I wouldn't think he would go back home? She probably isn't going with him for some other reason." Nikki commented.

"What would that be?" Jessica asked.

"That I don't know. But I think this is plan B. We must have done something to mess with plan A. Because he would have had her meet him somewhere. He isn't going to leave her behind." Daniel replied.

"They've been together too long for them to split up. They have a plan. We just need to figure it out." Nikki added.

"I think he's nervous, we have gotten closer to him than anyone has ever done. He's been exposed. He probably feels safer alone, or he may be regrouping, planning his next move. I do think Daniel is right though, this probably is plan B." Justin added.

"Let's think about this a minute. He takes his wife away from their home to her sister's. He leaves and ends up in Atlantic City. Then She goes back home. We're missing something. Let's say he planned on Elizabeth meeting him wherever he is. What would have changed that?" Daniel asked.

"Maybe he was supposed to meet up with her, but wanted her out of the way instead?" Jessica suggested.

"That's good, why would he want her out of the way?" Daniel continued.

"With her out of the way she would be safer. I mean since we are closer than he probably expected in his long term plan." Nikki suggested.

"Yes, that is quite possible. He most likely did plan this before we came along." Daniel continued to steer the conversation. "In that case then he is going to plan B, but what might that be?"

The four agents looked at one another. "Maybe he's planning to disappear." Justin exclaimed. "If that's the case we may not find him for a long time."

"Okay, say he is looking to disappear, killing a woman in Atlantic City isn't a good start." Jessica added.

"No it isn't, maybe he changed his plan after he killed her." Nikki suggested. "We were here pretty fast, that might have been the turning point."

"I think we might be onto something here. If he saw the newscast with us in it, he may have realized we are right behind him. So he got word to his wife to go home instead of meeting up with him.

So what does he do next then?" Daniel pushed to get more feedback from the team.

"He finds a way to get us off his trail." Nikki remarked.

"Yes. I agree, but what is he going to do?" Jessica added.

"He's going to stop us, maybe give us a false lead." Justin stated, speaking the first thoughts he had.

"Or," Nikki hesitated, remembering her dream where she felt enveloped by Lobo. "Maybe he will hunt us."

"That's a lot for him to take on. It would be suicide on his part." Daniel did not believe Lobo would take that route. After all perps run from the law, they don't go after it.

"Okay then, he wants to escape." Justin changed the subject realizing Daniel was very uncomfortable with the way it was going. "What ways could he do that?"

"He would have to leave his job, maybe go out of state?" Nikki responded.

"Where would he get money?" Jessica wondered. "Would his wife send it to him, or maybe he can access their account."

"Good points. He would have to pay rent and buy food, as well as other living expenses. He could have a stockpile of cash." Daniel suggested.

"Do you think he is in New Jersey?" Justin asked.

"Possible, but New York, Delaware, and Pennsylvania are all close." Nikki added.

"We really have no leads at this point. I have to check in with Albany tomorrow. If we don't come up with something we may have to put this guy aside until something else comes up. There are other cases that are fresh and need agents to take them over." Daniel was blunt. The others weren't happy with what he was saying but weren't surprised.

After lunch Daniel's phone rang. It was the state trooper from New Jersey he had spoken with a few days earlier. "Hey, something up?" Daniel listened intently; he looked up at the others and winked. "Okay, we'll meet you there, bye."

"These guys are relentless down here. They sat and watched every traffic camera they could over the last week. They believe they have him going over the Benjamin Franklin Bridge into Philadelphia." Daniel explained.

The mood in the room elevated, this was a lead. They hoped it was enough to keep them on the case. They went to the van and headed to the New Gretna State Police Barracks on the Parkway. When they arrived two troopers were waiting and escorted them into a room in the back. They watched the video feed, it was a clear picture. "He drove across the bridge at six-thirty in the morning. There isn't much traffic at that time on a Sunday morning. When he paid the toll the camera took a clear picture of the plate and the driver."

The four agents practically fell over one another to get a look. "That's him. It's definitely him." Jessica remarked.

"We have a plate! Did you guys run it?" Daniel asked.

"We certainly did, but it's registered to a corporation." The trooper then went on. "We gave it to the Philadelphia Police

Department to keep a look out for it, but they haven't gotten back to us yet."

"The Oak Tree Land Development Corporation, I suspect?" Daniel stated.

"Yes, I believe that's it." The trooper acknowledged.

"That's who this guy works or worked for. There is no doubt that it's him. At least we have a plate now. With some luck someone will notice it." Justin remarked.

After spending about a half hour talking about the case and thanking the troopers for their help, the agents decided to go back and check out of their motel and head into Philadelphia."

CHAPTER THIRTEEN

Lobo spent the week keeping up with the news and calling hotels and motels around Atlantic City to find out if the FBI was still in the area. When he called the High Roller Inn on Wednesday, pretending to be a reporter, he was led to believe they were still there. He was a little relieved by that, he knew where they were, and it wasn't Philly.

Friday late afternoon Lobo noticed his phone flashing. He looked at the message, it was from Matt Newman. "I thought I would have heard from him sooner." He thought out loud. He pushed the view button on his phone.

"Hey brother, not sure what's going on with you. If you need time off that's fine. Let me know when you want to get back to work. The New Jersey Troopers called here concerning the car you have. They wanted to know who was driving it last weekend. We told them we couldn't find the records for that particular car. But they said that it was an urgent matter."

"Fuck!" Was all he could think of at that moment. He sent a text back to Matt. "Over did things in Atlantic City. Need a vacation, thanks."

He took a deep breath and put his head back, looking at the ceiling. "This is getting too complicated." He said knowing had to either get rid of the car, the plates, or both.

He checked the amount of money he had in the false bottom of the night stand in the bedroom. A little over five thousand dollars in cash. "I should have saved more." He said to himself.

He planned to go and find a cheap second hand car on Saturday morning. But first he would take his car, minus his belongings, and drop it off in a bad part of town once it was dark.

That night he took the SUV and put it in a parking lot north of where he was living. He then walked back to his apartment. It was close to one in the morning when he got home. He then texted his friend. "Matt, I'm sorry but the car was stolen, it was gone when I went to go to the store!"

He had met Matt when he was twenty-two years old back in 2001. Matt was in school at Penn State and was out with some buddies for the weekend. They ended up in Wilkes-Barre where he and Elizabeth had been living. Lobo met Matt when he went out for a drink, they hit it off from the start. When Matt graduated and began to work for his father he had remembered how Lobo loved the country and thought he might like a job. Lobo started working there and did not let Matt down. He became one of their top scouts, he was able to broker better deals than the other scouts and made quite a bit of money for the company. The choice Matt made in hiring Lobo is what aided Matt to be his father's choice to take over the company when he retired.

He knew Matt would follow up with the report. At least he would not be connected to the car any longer. Hopefully it would clear him as a suspect. However he had a feeling it was too late for that.

Matt received Lobo's text, he snickered. He knew Lobo was on the wild side. However he did not know the truth about Lobo's life. If he had, he would never have had anything to do with him.

The next morning Matt reported the car stolen, no questions were asked.

~ ~ ~ ~ ~ ~ ~

Friday evening the agents checked into the Hawthorne Inn which was in the Center City section of Philadelphia. Daniel liked staying at that particular chain of motels. They were reasonable and kept the rooms clean.

Daniel contacted the local police once they were settled in their room and explained who they were and why they were there. The Philadelphia Police were aware of the bulletin posted for the SUV and the license plate number from the New Jersey State Troopers.

Saturday morning Daniel received a call from the Philadelphia Police Department. When he got off the phone he sat on his bed, put his hands to his face, and then bent over with his elbows on his knees.

“What is it Daniel?” Justin knew something was seriously wrong.

Daniel sat up, looked at Justin. "Get the girls, we'll talk about it together."

Justin knocked on the door adjoining their rooms. "Something's wrong, get in here!"

Nikki and Jessica were still in their pajamas, they put on their robes and entered into Daniel and Justin's room.

"I got a call from the Philadelphia Police Department. They found the car Lobo was driving."

"That's great! Where is he?" Jessica was excited, not sensing the gravity in Daniels body language.

Nikki did however. "Jessica, I don't think its good news."

"No, it really isn't. It was found in a rough part of the city. A patrol car found it. Realizing it was not the type of car that should be in that area he ran the plates. It came up first that the car was of interest, and then that it was reported stolen by the Oak Tree Land Development Corporation."

"Are you kidding me!" Justin exclaimed.

“Are they protecting him?” Jessica questioned.

“He found out that we had his plate and car identified. He dumped the car and then called the company. They probably don’t know the entire picture.” Nikki remarked.

“How did he find out? Has it been in the paper or on the news?” Daniel questioned.

“I haven’t seen it on the news. I’ve been watching what they’re reporting. Only the local law enforcement knew about the plates. Oh yea, they did call the Land Development Corporation, remember?” Justin recalled.

“Then he must have been tipped off by someone at the company.” Daniel noted.

“It’s pointless to go looking for who tipped him off, right now anyway.” Nikki stated. “He probably won’t tell them where he’s staying.”

“She’s right!” Daniel added.

"He's in Philadelphia. After he dropped off the car he went somewhere on foot or by public transportation. He won't trust anyone right now to involve them. He is in Philadelphia!" Nikki exclaimed.

The other three looked at Nikki, she was sure about this. "That would make sense, Nikki, let's find out exactly where the car was found and see what's around it." Daniel directed.

It was early afternoon when Daniel and the team pulled up to the spot where Lobo's car was found. Looking around Daniel remarked, "He chose a very bad area to dump the car. It would appear like it was stolen by someone from this part of town, if you didn't know better."

Nikki took out the map of Philadelphia and located the area they were in. "It looks like south of here is a relatively nice area. There's a couple of colleges, it's marked as University City on the map. North seems like it gets worse. East is Center City and west is West Chester. Before that is a river, the zoo, and highways. Not a very likely area. My guess is either Center City or near University City."

"Any thoughts?" Daniel opened it up to discussion.

"All I have to say is that if it's University City there are a lot of young women there. We better find him soon." Jessica was worried about more victims. It was like putting a fox in a hen house, the thought of Lobo near college students.

"I kind of think it would be University City over Center City. Center City is just too crowded." Justin reasoned.

"I agree." Nikki felt that University City was also the most likely.

"Okay then, how should we handle this?" Daniel again looked for a discussion.

"First of all we should have the campus police and Philadelphia police involved. We can give them a copy of the sketch so they can keep watch for him." Jessica was still concerned about the college students.

"The more eyes we have the better." Justin agreed.

“What do you think, Nikki?” Daniel asked.

“I think we should set a trap for him, lore him out.” Nikki was thinking. “We need to plant a story in the paper, or on the news. False information of some kind. Or make him think something happened to Elizabeth, he would come out of hiding for her!”

“That’s either the craziest thing I ever heard, or the best idea. I’m not sure which?” Justin wasn’t sure what to think about her idea, it wasn’t what they normally would do.

“It’s drastic, but we are in a desperate situation. I’ll think about it.” Daniel said not wanting to alienate Nikki, or make her feel awkward.

“I know it sounds crazy. I’m a little frantic that’s all. I won’t be upset if you don’t want to do it. I realized after I said it that it was off the wall.” Nikki knew she had gone too far. It was her lack of experience as an FBI agent, along with the emotional strain she was under with this case. She would do anything to get this guy, even break the rules if it would work.

They drove around University City and the surrounding area. There were many places that had for rent signs due to the college students being nearby. “This really isn’t going to get us anywhere. It’s just too vast of an area. Let’s head back to the motel and talk to the local authorities like Jessica suggested.”

Once they were at the motel Daniel called to check in with his superiors in Albany. When he returned to the motel room the team was waiting to hear if there were any new developments. “They want us to take a break. We’ve been working this case for going on three weeks nonstop. Next weekend we have to take a four day weekend. Once we return we can continue the case.”

“What if he kills someone else? How can we live with that?” Jessica questioned.

“I don’t think he will. We are pressing hard and he knows it. He will lay low for awhile. Albany agrees and thinks this is the best time for us to take a break.” Daniel explained.

“We have a week, between now and Friday. Who knows what will happen.” Justin wanted to give them a little hope.

"I'm going to call the authorities like Jessica suggested earlier. You guys order some pizza and wings. We'll eat and go from there." Daniel stepped into the other room to make his call.

The rest of the day was uneventful. The Philadelphia Police and campus police agreed to circulate the sketch and keep an eye out for the perp. They would call if anything came up.

That night Nikki dreamt again, but this time it was different. She was walking side by side with the man in her dream. She was happy and felt fulfilled. She saw red rose pedals falling around her and dreamt she could smell the sweet rose scent. When she started to wake up she felt her inner self screaming, "NO!" She didn't want to leave the dream.

~~~~~~~~~~

Lobo also dreamt. He dreamt about the woman haunting him. He saw her in his dream; instead of being allusive she turned and walked toward him. She was holding a rose and dropping the petals as she went. Soon all around him were rose petals floating down from the sky. He picked one up, it turned to blood and
~~~~~~~~~~

dripped to the ground where it turned back into a rose petal. The woman was then standing in front of him. She put her hand out summoning him to come to her. He woke and sat up in bed. "What the Hell." He rubbed his face and ran his fingers through his hair, then he laid back down. It took awhile but he fell back to sleep.

Sunday morning Lobo went to the corner store and purchased a Sunday paper and cup of coffee. Once he returned home he read the paper while drinking his coffee. In one of the back sections there was information about New Jersey and the casino's. There was an article about the missing woman. The reporter stated that the FBI left New Jersey for Philadelphia, that they were following a lead there.

Lobo smiled. He saw this as Nikki coming to him, more than he felt they were getting closer to him. He looked at the name of the reporter, Jennifer Greyson, he felt she could help him find Nikki.

Monday morning he would give Jennifer Greyson a call as a concerned reporter of a magazine which he would figure out later.

Maybe she could help him find their motel. Then it would just be a matter of time till he separated Nikki from the other three and silenced her.

~ ~ ~ ~ ~ ~ ~ ~ ~ ~

Sunday came and went for the agents. They spent most of the day hoping for a phone call that would give them a lead. They discussed the case till there was nothing else to talk about. Nikki was awkwardly silent and it was noticed by Jessica. "What's wrong?" She asked when the guys were out of ear shot.

"Nothing really. I had a restless sleep and I'm just a little disturbed that we can't seem to get close to this guy. Maybe we do need a break? A fresh start might be good." Nikki was starting to think she really needed a break from thinking about Lobo day and night. Then maybe the dreams would stop.

Daniel and Justin came back into the room. "What's up?" Daniel realized they were having a serious conversation.

"Nikki was just saying that a break might help the case, it might give us all a fresh perspective." Jessica replied.

"I was thinking the same thing." Daniel replied. "I had that happen once before. I was a state trooper then, we took a weekend off and when we came back together we saw something that we hadn't noticed before."

"I do feel a little burnt out." Justin admitted.

"Let's take the rest of the night off, go down to the bar have dinner and a drink." Jessica suggested.

They all agreed.

~~~~~~~~~~

Monday morning Lobo called the Philadelphia Press and asked to speak to Jennifer Greyson. "Jennifer speaking, can I help you?"

"Hello Jennifer, my name is Lawrence Mohar. I work for a men's magazine called Men's Quarterly. I have been following your articles about the missing woman in Atlantic City. I was wondering if you knew where I could find the FBI agents who were working on the case. I was thinking of writing an article about them for the next issue."
~~~~~~~~~~

"I would be happy to help a fellow journalist. I heard they were at the Hawthorne Inn outside of Center City. Good luck, I tried to get an interview and they turned me down."

"Thanks for the heads up, and thank you for the help." Lobo was truly thankful to her.

"Sure thing, take care." She replied as she hung up.

Lobo had what he needed. Now how to take care of his problem. He knew that she would most likely be sharing a room with the other woman agent. He decided to watch their routine and take it from there. He drove over to the Hawthorne Inn and waited in the parking lot to see if he could catch a glimpse of them.

When he arrived at the motel it wasn't hard to figure out what vehicle was theirs. He spent every day of the week watching. The most he saw was one of the men taking the van out and coming back with a couple of grocery bags. Friday afternoon however the four agents came out together with suitcases. They placed the luggage in the van and then talked for a few minutes. The one woman then hugged Nikki as the three got into the van.

“I’ll see you Monday!” Nikki called as the van drove off. She then returned to the motel.

Hearing what Nikki had said, Lobo got out of his car and followed behind her to see where she went. She got into the elevator, he knew there were only two floors. He took the stairs that were next to the elevator. When he arrived on the second floor he peeked out the door and saw Nikki walking down the hall. She stopped and opened the door with a key card and entered the room. He quickly walked down the hall to see the room number, then turned and went back down to the first floor. He went out to his car and waited.

Nikki had decided to stay at the motel and rest for the weekend. The other three had friends and relatives near Albany and were looking forward to seeing them. Nikki, however, did not want to return home until she had caught the killer of her friend. It was a pact she had made with herself. She returned to her room rented a pay per view movie and drank a couple glasses of wine before falling asleep.

Lobo decided he would make himself known to the night shift when they arrived at work. He went into the motel, greeted the desk clerk and proceeded to talk with her about the weather and other forms of small talk before going into the bar for a drink. He watched the hockey game on the big screen TV with the rest of the crowd. The Phillies were playing a home game, it was exciting to see the crowd cheer them on to their win. It was eleven o'clock by the time the game was over. He went to the desk clerk he had greeted earlier. "Hi, I forgot the key card to my room. Do you have an extra?"

"Yes sir we do, what is your room number?"

"It's room 214."

The clerk went to a drawer and pulled out a key card. "This should work, please return it in the morning."

"No problem, thank you." Lobo turned to use the elevator, he was looking forward to this. He could feel his heart start to race with excitement.

He walked down the hallway and put the card into the slot, the door opened, he entered the room as quietly as possible. It was lit by the light of the television. He looked over and saw that Nikki was asleep on the bed next to the window. He reached down and pulled his knife out of its holster strapped around his lower leg.

He began to walk over to the bed where she was lying. He could see her face in the dim light. As he looked at her he began to remember his dreams, the feelings that he had felt within them and realized that he was connected to this woman. He didn't understand it, but he knew he would not be able to harm her. He walked over to the bed and leaned on it with one knee. He dropped the knife on the floor as he leaned toward her.

Nikki felt the bed move as he pushed on the mattress with his knee. She opened her eyes slightly.

"Hello Nikki!" He said as he leaned toward her. She wasn't fully awake and thought for a minute that she was dreaming. Realizing that she wasn't dreaming but was awake and that Lobo was in her motel room, and on her bed, she started to sit up as a reflex action.

He pushed her back down holding her arms above her head. “Let me go, what do you think you’re doing?” Nikki said struggling against him.

“I came here to stop you from finding me. To put an end to this cat and mouse game we’ve been playing in our dreams. When I entered your room I was going to kill you. Without you the other three would never catch me. That was until I got close to you.” He let go of her arm with his right hand and stroked her face and hair.

Nikki was listening to what he was saying, not quite sure what to do. He had her pinned down, and she couldn’t move.

“But then I realized that I can’t kill the other half of myself? I felt it the closer I got to you. The dreams that I’ve been having they have all been about you, were connected.”

Nikki lay looking up at the man she had hated and wanted to destroy, and asked. “What dreams?”

"You've been invading my dreams almost nightly. Before I even realized it was you. Haunting me, pulling out emotions deep within me that I never felt before." Lobo confessed.

Nikki realized that she wasn't afraid. She felt a strange closeness, and calmness with the situation. "I've had dreams too, dreams that I couldn't face. Afraid of what they meant. I suspected it was you in those dreams. Now I know it was!" Nikki was drawn away from reality, she wasn't in control any longer. Having Lobo this close to her gave him a strange power over her.

He looked into her eyes, leaned toward her and kissed her lips. To his surprise she responded.

She was overcome by the deep attraction to him that had begun stirring from her dreams.

As he felt her follow his lead and stop resisting, he released the hold he had on her. He slid his hand down her side, under her pajama shirt and into her underwear. She responded to him at each step, he could feel her breathing deepen as he ran his hand just past her breasts, her muscles relaxed and her legs slightly opened as he put his hand into her pants. He slowly slid his fingers between her layers of skin till he found what he was looking for. She gasped as he pushed his finger inside her.

She was warm and moist, he slid his finger out of her and moved slightly upward. She moaned as he gently rubbed and circled the soft area that slowly became more prominent and erect.

She reached down and attempted to remove her underwear, he likewise removed his pants. They came back together and looked into the face of the other in the light of the television. Without a word they leaned toward one another and kissed. Lobo then moved down to her neck, and to her right breast.

Nikki could barely contain the ecstasy she felt pulsating through her entire body. She held him close as he pulled himself on top of her, pushed her legs apart with his knee and pushed himself inside her.

She was excited, eager, and yearned for him. Nikki felt herself surrendering to him, she began sliding into another level of consciousness as she felt him inside her.

After a few minutes he lifted himself up on his knees and reached down to rub her sensitive spot with his finger as he continued to move in and out of her. He watched as she moaned and whimpered under the touch of his hand. As he watched her facial expressions he knew that he had control over her body. It reminded him of the women who had surrendered to him as he took their life away, slowly sliding his knife into them. The feeling he got as he felt their life slowly drain away while he held them, he was in control then too.

She let out a moan and he felt her pulsate inside as she started to cum. The warm gush coming from her was too much for him and he could no longer hold out. He collapsed on top of her with a grunt, helpless as he too reached orgasm.

He lay on top of her until his penis fell out from inside of her. He then rolled to her side and pulled her to him. He kissed her, wrapped his arms around her, and they fell asleep in each other's arms.

CHAPTER FOURTEEN

The sun was up when Nikki opened her eyes. It took a second for her to remember where she was, and who she as with. She looked at the man whom she had hated. For a second her mind began to grasp the situation she was in. She quickly pushed that reality away, she wasn't able to face the situation.

Lobo looked into her eyes, leaned forward and kissed her on the lips. As he kissed her neck, he could feel her breathing change. He then kissed her on her chest and then on her nipple. He was completely drawn to her and felt he would never be able to get enough of her body. As he touched her breasts and nipples he could feel her yielding herself to his touch. He moved his hand down, pushed her legs apart and touched her sensitive spot, she gasped in ecstasy. He could feel the swollen, hardened nodule of skin that was the key to her arousal.

His touch caused her to forget everything except what he was doing, with his kiss she felt herself melting into submission. She felt him separate her skin folds to find her clitoris, and heard herself gasp as he did. She was completely lost in ecstasy as he pushed his finger inside her and barely heard the guttural sound that came out of her.

He turned her onto her stomach and push her onto her knees. As he pushed himself inside of her she groaned.

The sensation was overwhelming to her. She called his name as he reached under her abdomen and began to rub her bulging clitoris. She felt herself losing her identity as he pushed her further and further toward orgasm.

He felt her quivering body beneath him as he reached beneath her to rub her sensitive spot. She was so moist and tight inside. He lost control and came within a few minutes of entering her. He pushed her onto her side as he kept himself inside her. She was still excited, writhing under his touch. He rubbed her until she exploded. He continued to rub as she tried to push him away but he was stronger and held onto her. Continuing to rub her with his finger, he knew that she was extremely sensitive now that she had climaxed. He could feel her ecstasy turn to sexual pain, she grabbed at his hand trying to pull his finger away from her. She mumbled, “Stop, please stop.” Instead he continued to rub her. He rolled her onto her back, wrapped his elbows behind her knees and pulled her legs back toward her head. He then pushed himself into her. She let out a yell as her flesh tore when he pushed into her.

He knew it would take him awhile to finish, since he had done so not long before. He relaxed and enjoyed the act of pushing in and out of her.

Nikki lay on her back pinned, unable to move. She was still feeling the aftermath of her orgasm, as he entered her. The tearing of her vaginal area was painful and pleasurable at the same time. She yelled out as he entered her. Now she lay waiting for him to finish. It seemed to take hours instead of minutes as her body was no longer excited causing his actions to become more uncomfortable with each thrust. Suddenly she felt him push one last time, deep within her. He released her legs when his orgasm was finished and lay on top of her.

She straightened her legs out, as he rolled over and lay next to her.

He pulled her to him, holding her tight as he whispered. "I need you Nikki."

Nikki had been with other men, three to be exact. This was not her first sexual experience. None of the other men she had been with came anywhere close to fulfilling her. She left each relationship emotionally drained, hurt, and sexually unfulfilled.

This was the first time she met someone who could cause her to feel so helpless by their touch. She felt as though every part of her had been violated. But at the same time she welcomed his every touch. She thought of Elizabeth as she lay in the arms of her husband. She wondered if he was like this with her. She pushed the thoughts aside as the reality of her situation again became too real.

Lobo had fallen asleep. Nikki laid awake thinking of his words and feeling the sensations that were coming from her body. She was sore. The spot where her skin had ripped was now beginning to burn as her own body fluids came in contact with the area. She wanted to get a shower to stop the burning. She attempted to slip out of the bed.

"Where are you going?" Lobo said half awake.

"I need to get a shower." She answered.

"Alright." Lobo replied as he rolled over to his other side letting go of Nikki so she could get out of the bed.

Once in the bathroom Nikki turned on the shower, waited for it to warm up and stepped inside. After washing her hair and face she began to wash herself between her legs, carefully dabbing herself with the wash cloth so it wouldn't hurt. She wasn't having much luck. She gave up on using the washcloth and put soap onto her fingers and gently used them to wash herself. She was sore and raw, but it felt good, even fulfilling. As she cleansed herself she remembered what he was doing to her that caused the rawness and the tear. As she put the two together she started to feel herself getting excited again.

She stopped cleansing herself and stood allowing the warm water to run over her back, it felt nice, comforting. As she stood in the shower she felt reality entering her mind, this was the man who had brutally killed her best friend. All of a sudden a pain gripped her very soul. She held her abdomen in an attempt to control it. She began to cry, to sob almost uncontrollably. She quickly regained herself as she heard a noise and noticed the shower curtain being pulled back. She turned and saw that it was Lobo pulling the curtain back.

She pushed him with both her hands, got out of the shower and began to pound him on the chest as she yelled. "You killed my best friend!"

He grabbed her by the arms without saying a word, wrapped her in a towel, picked her up and carried her back to the bed. He laid her down, grabbed her jaw and turned her face toward him. "I'm so sorry Nikki, I didn't know. I would never purposely hurt you. Do you understand that?"

Nikki looked up at him, he seemed so sincere, and she believed him. "Yes, I do. But why do you do it? I don't understand."

He looked deep into her eyes. He had never talked to anyone about his dark desires. Not even Elizabeth, even though she knew. "I don't know? It's just an urge, like sex, it builds up until I need to release it."

"Why did you start?" She had so many questions to ask him, she wanted to understand.

"There was this girl, she was liked by everyone at school. The other boys wanted to take her out on dates, or talked about wanting to get to third base with her. I just wanted to hurt her. That was the first time I had the urge. I followed her until one night she was alone and I killed her. It felt good."

Nikki wanted to keep talking about this with him, but at the same time she didn't want to hear anymore.

He stroked her wet hair tenderly. "I have you now Nikki, you make me feel so whole. I haven't felt like this since I was a very young boy."

Nikki looked at him, listening to what he was saying. Unable to fully grasp exactly what this meant for her, but had a good idea what it meant for other women who otherwise would be his victims.

As he looked into her eyes, searching her soul he knew she trusted him, but it wasn't enough. He wanted more than that, he needed to have her completely to himself. He had to possess her very soul. It was the only way he could ensure his safety and to keep her in his life.

He removed the wet towel from around her and covered her naked body with blankets. "Get some rest, I'm going to go wash up." He kissed her on the forehead before heading into the bathroom.

Nikki fell asleep shortly after she heard him go into the bathroom.

After his shower Lobo decided to go to the convenience store that was across the street from the motel. For a small convenience type store it had quite an assortment of breakfast items. As he walked up and down the aisles he noticed other things that he thought would be useful. He brought back coffee, bagels and muffins. He used his key card to get back into the room, Nikki was still asleep. He put down the bags on the table and stood watching her sleep.

He noticed his knife on the floor slightly under the bed where he had dropped it after realizing he would kill himself before he would ever be able to kill this woman. He picked it up, removed the holster on his leg and put it into the leather holster. He then placed it into the drawer of the table next to the bed.

He sat in the chair across from the bed watching Nikki sleep. He thought that she was the most beautiful thing he had ever seen. But he knew that he couldn't trust her completely yet. He felt she was loyal to the other three agents and to her friend. He wanted her to be loyal to him, and only him, he wanted to own her. He felt there was only one way to make that happen.

When Nikki woke up, she looked over and saw Lobo sleeping in the chair across from her. She also saw coffee and white plastic bags on the table. She was curious as to what he had bought. She got out of bed and put on her bathrobe. She then looked into one of the bags and saw a couple of bagels, cream cheese, and muffins. She pulled out a crème filled muffin, put cream and sugar in one of the coffees and sat at the table enjoying the breakfast he had provided her.

Once she was finished she approached Lobo sitting in the chair, she sat on his lap. He woke up and smiled. “Good morning beautiful.”

Nikki leaned toward him and kissed him gently on his lips. They snuggled in the chair. Nikki could hear his heart beat as she laid her head on his chest. It was comforting to her.

Lobo enjoyed the time holding her, he felt whole and fulfilled. Then he took her hand and pushed it between the flaps of the bathrobe she was wearing toward her pubic area. “I want you to make yourself cum.” He told her.

Nikki was not prone to self-arousal and was a little uncomfortable at his request. She moved her hand away.

He again pushed her hand toward her pubic area and repeated himself. “I want to watch you make yourself cum.”

Nikki continued to passively resist.

He stood up with her in his arms, carried her over to the bed and laid her down. Kneeling next to her bed he opened up her bathrobe. He then took her hand and put it down on her private area. He leaned toward her ear. “Make yourself cum for me.”

Nikki was uncomfortable with his request but also wanted to please him, she closed her eyes and hesitatingly began to rub her clitoris.

“That’s my girl he whispered.”

He watched as Nikki did as he had told her. After a few minutes he kissed and sucked on her nipples. By her breathing he knew that she was close to orgasm. He reached down and pulled her hand away before she came.

She looked up at him wondering why he stopped her.

He then stood up, removed his pants and sat next to her on the bed. He took his hand and put it on the back of her head and pushed her face toward himself.

Nikki knew what he wanted, she began to suck on him. He laid back on the bed to allow her to do what she wanted to him. Nikki was glad he changed the direction of their love making. She was more comfortable with this than she was with pleasuring herself.

After a few minutes he pulled her off of him. Pushed her onto her stomach and kissed her back. He moved down to her buttocks and kissed each cheek. He then took his finger and attempted to push it into her rectum.

Nikki pulled away not wanting any type of anal sex as he attempted to put his finger into her. He put his leg over hers, and the upper half of his body across her back. He attempted again to put his finger into her rectum.

She squirmed beneath him saying. "Stop I don't want to do that!"

Lobo whispered. "Relax, you'll love it. I promise!"

Nikki knew she had no choice. He was stronger than her and would be able to do whatever he wanted. She relaxed only to save herself pain and allowed him to put his finger into her.

He was gentle. He slowly pushed his finger in and out of her as he concentrated on her breathing and listened to her every sound.

After a few minutes he stopped, then got up and stepped away from the bed.

Nikki lay watching as he went over to the table and picked up something from the other white plastic bag. She rolled onto her side, facing him as he returned to the bed.

He knelt on the floor and looked into her eyes. "I want you to belong to me Nikki." He stroked her hair and ran his thumb across her cheek. "I need you."

He stood and began to push her back onto her stomach. Nikki resisted. "You don't have to do this!"

He put the jar of petroleum jelly on the table next to the bed. Removing the lid he put his fingers into the contents. He then pushed Nikki the rest of the way onto her stomach. Wiping the lubricant on Nikki's anus he pushed two of his fingers in her at the same time.

Nikki groaned as she felt him push his two fingers into her. She felt herself stretch, and tried to relax so it wouldn't be painful. She was partially successful, the pain she felt was lessened once he had successfully pushed both fingers in as far as they would go. The pain then turned more on the side of pleasure as he gently moved them within her.

He rolled her onto her left side, and continued to push his fingers in and out of her. He laid next to her with his one arm under her, holding her near him.

After he felt she was stretched enough, he pulled his two fingers out. He replenished the petroleum jelly that had melted away and pushed a third finger into her. She let out a yelp and he could feel her tremble. He kissed the back of her head and asked, "Are you alright?"

"No! Please don't do this!" Nikki begged. She could feel her rectum being stretched. It was painful no matter how much she tried to relax.

Lobo stopped moving his fingers and just left them inside of her. "Rub yourself, Nikki."

Nikki heard him and felt a tear drip from her eye. "Please." She repeated over and over, "Please, please."

He could hear the tone in her voice, she was helpless and knew it. He felt so drawn to her, she was almost his, totally and completely. He ignored her, he knew he had to break her, he had to own her in order to trust her with his life. "Rub yourself like you did earlier, it won't hurt so much if you do."

Out of self-preservation Nikki moved her hand from her side to between her legs. She reached for herself and began to rub.

"That's my girl. Go slow, don't make yourself cum. Just excite yourself." He smiled as he knew he had won.

Nikki did as he instructed her. She could feel him once again begin to move his fingers slowly in and out of her. He was being as gently as he could, it didn't hurt as bad. He took his time, stretching her and relaxing her muscles before he took his hand away and reached for more lubricant.

She felt him pull his fingers out and hoped he was done, she started to move her hand from between her legs.

"Don't stop." He whispered. He took another handful of petroleum jelly from the container and rubbed it around and within her. He also put some on himself. He then pushed her onto her stomach. Climbing onto her, he slowly pushed himself into her rectum. She was so tight, he loved every sensation he felt. He also loved the sounds he was hearing Nikki make, the guttural animal sound excited him. He watched as she grabbed the pillow with her fingers and tightly squeezed it, raised her head slightly off the pillow with her mouth open, grunting continuously as he slowly pushed fully into her. He stopped once he was in as deep as he could go. He was being as gentle as he could, he didn't really want to hurt her but he did want to consume her, and only knew one way to do that.

Nikki felt him rub the jelly on and in her, and knew what he was going to do next. She began to rub herself faster, she wanted to be as excited as she possibly could be to prepare for the inevitable. As he lowly pushed inside her she let out a scream, out of reflex she grabbed the pillow under her head with her other hand. She felt herself stretched beyond what she was able to endure. Her only release was what she could verbalize. She felt him stop and be still within her. She also felt her tissue throbbing as it was pushed to its extreme.

He lay on top of her for quite awhile before he began to slowly push in and out of her. As he did he whispered into Nikki's ear, "You belong to me. Tell me your mine!"

Nikki shuddered inside her soul, she knew it was true. Between her grunts and moans she answered him. "I belong to you… I belong to you!"

He continued to enjoy himself until he came. He pulled out of her and pushed her onto her back. "Make yourself cum for me." He whispered in her ear.

"Okay, I will… I will." She answered as she rubbed herself until she reached orgasm.

"That's my girl." He said as she came.

Nikki rolled onto her side with her back toward him.

He lay next to her with his arm around her. "You're perfect for me." He said. They laid in silence. Lobo thinking of his conquest while Nikki was numb, trying to come to grips with what was happening to her.

As she lay next to him, she could tell he had fallen asleep by the way he was breathing. She cried silently horrified by what she had experienced but not wanting him to hear. She was in shock, the last 24 hours had changed her completely and she knew it. She was lying next to a monster, she grasped that much. She also knew she didn't want to be away from him. "What is wrong with me?" She thought. She felt safe with his arms around her and his leg over her. She loved the feeling of being near him and knew she had a connection with him. "What is wrong with me?" She again thought as she began to realize what this man had done to her physically, emotionally and to her very soul.

Nikki barely recognized her own name as she thought of herself. He had stripped her identity from her, who was she? Where would she go from here? How could she face Daniel? Daniel. She had been attracted to him and hoped he was to her also, that seemed so far away now. Her allegiance to him and the rest of the team was a blank. She couldn't seem to connect with any of them. She tried to think of Jessica, they had become friends, she struggled to emotionally connect to her, and she couldn't. She let out an uncontrollable sob as she tried to face what had happened to her. She became afraid as she realized Lobo had heard her and was waking up.

"Nikki?" He was groggy but knew something was wrong with her. "What's going on?" She didn't answer him.

Nikki lay totally still, afraid to move, she hoped he would think she was asleep.

Lobo rose up on his elbow and looked at her, and then at the clock on the table. It was after midnight but the room was bright in the light from the lamps. He reached to turn off the light switch that was next to the bed. The room was still lit by the light from the television screen, the dim light was better for him. He picked up the remote from the table and began changing the channels until he found the twenty-four hour news. He relaxed with his head on two pillows so he could comfortably see the television screen over Nikki's head.

Nikki lay pretending to be asleep. She didn't know how to act, or what to say to him. Earlier it was easy, despite who he was she wanted to be near him. Now she didn't know what she wanted. She was confused, scared, and wanted nothing more than to cry, she couldn't even do that with him near her.

As she lay there she suddenly had an uncontrollable urge to jump up and get away from him, but then what? She fought the feeling until it was gone. She couldn't control the sob that suddenly erupted from her. She was horrified as she realized that he heard her. When he moved she rolled onto her back, she could no longer control her emotions. She covered her face as the uncontrollable sobs started coming.

Lobo heard Nikki sob, he looked down at her then sat up allowing Nikki to roll onto her back. He saw her lower lip quiver as she covered her face with her hands and started to sob uncontrollably. He realized he had gone too far.

CHAPTER FIFTEEN

Daniel, Justin, and Jessica arrived in Albany at three in the afternoon on Friday. After parking the van, Jessica and Justin walked to their own vehicles and went their separate ways for the weekend. Jessica had a fiancée she hadn't seen and Justin hadn't been away from his wife and two children this long in quite awhile.

Daniel headed into the FBI office to speak with his superior.

"Hi Francine, how have you been?" Daniel greeted Francine Dapper as he walked down the hallway to Robert Miller's office.

"Hi Daniel, any new leads on the case?" Francine asked.

"No, unfortunately. This is a tough one."

"You'll get him, you always do." Francine replied as she turned to walk down the hall.

Daniel knocked on Robert's door. "Come on in Daniel." He was able to see part of Daniel's face through the small window in the door.

Daniel entered the room and shook hands with his friend and boss. "I'm afraid that I don't have anything new to bring to you Bob."

"What's the problem with this one?" Robert asked, knowing Daniel would have an answer. He was on top of every situation he was ever in, and this one would be no different.

"It seems that the odds are always in this guy's favor. Even when he makes a mistake he somehow comes out on top. I can't explain it! He must have found out we had photos of him in his car. The next thing we hear is that the car was found abandoned, and on top of that reported stolen by the company that owned it!" Daniel confessed.

Daniel sat down in a chair next to Robert's desk. "We can't get close enough to him. That's the bottom line. It's like he can sense when we're near. We showed up a few hours after he left his house, and the same at his sister-in-law's! If it wasn't for Nikki and the connection she seems to have with the way this guy thinks, we wouldn't have even gotten as close as we did. She's like a hound on a scent, she's driven. I'm lucky to have her on my team."

"What's her take right now on where this guy is?" Robert was curious.

"She's as frustrated and tired as the rest of us. I think she might be starting to grasp at straws. At the last meeting she thought that he might be hunting our team instead of running from us."

"Would that fit his profile, is it possible? Did you think about it?" Robert asked.

Daniel looked at his friend, slightly confused by his question. "No, that doesn't happen with these guys! They are the prey not the hunters."

"Their also hunters. I don't believe it has ever happened before, but maybe we should consider what she was saying. You said it yourself that she has a connection to this guy."

"Well, if he's turning the tables on us we can consider setting a trap and wait for him to show up." The suggestion from Bob started to make Daniel think. "It won't hurt at this point to consider her suggestion. If she's right we'll be ready. If he doesn't show, we'll go to Georgia until we get another lead." Daniel had a plan in place in his head, he would share it with the team when they were together again.

"I want this guy as bad as you and your team. It's been close to four weeks that we've been looking for him. But if the trail stays cold, and there aren't any new developments in the next few days, we're going to have to put him aside till we have a lead. There are two other killers out there. One in Nebraska, and one in Georgia. I would like for you and the team to go to Georgia. All the evidence isn't in, but it looks like something is going on down there." Robert knew Daniel hated failure, and didn't want him to see this as failure, just a detour.

"I know we can't keep going in circles here. Just promise me you'll give it to my team the next time this guy surfaces." Daniel requested.

"I wouldn't trust him to anyone else!" Robert had full trust in Daniel and his team.

The two men stood and shook hands as Daniel left to return home for the weekend. He was looking forward to relaxing alone for a couple days. He wasn't surprised by what Bob had said, he expected it. He and the other agents who hunt these types of people close cases in a week, two at the most. This one was now going on for a month. He also knew that the few who elude them for a longer period of time are usually the ones who make headlines. That was the last thing he wanted.

The weekend flew by for Daniel, Jessica and Justin. They met back in the parking lot Monday morning at eight for the ride back to Philadelphia. Once on the road Daniel asked Jessica to text Nikki and let her know they would be arriving about two o'clock.

A few minutes later Jessica received a text back. "Okay, see you then."

~~~~~~~~~~
~~~~~~~~~~

Lobo sat next to Nikki, after a few minutes she calmed down and rolled back onto her side. He reached over to put his hand on her shoulder, she startled, then lay still.

"Nikki, Nikki? Look at me." He waited but Nikki remained motionless. He then pushed her shoulder toward him so that she would be on her back. He then touched her cheek with the back of his other hand, rubbing her cheek gently. "I went too far, I'm sorry. Please look at me."

Nikki slowly opened her eyes. She knew he would keep at her until she did. It was hard for her to look at him, to face him after what he had done to her. She wished he had killed her physically, rather than killing her soul. She felt dead inside, she didn't know who she was anymore and that scared her. She looked into his eyes apprehensively, not knowing how to react to him, or how he would react to her. She never felt so aware of how defenseless she was. His eyes seemed empty, and cold. She could only look for a second before closing her eyes and turning her head.

He could see a mixture of shame and fear in her eyes, once she turned away he knew he had to win her back. He walked into the bathroom and turned on the water in the sink. While waiting for the water to warm up, he picked up a washcloth and soap along with a dry towel.

Nikki felt him leave the bed, she pulled the sheet over her as the tears welled up in her eyes.

When he returned he sat on the bed and gently pulled the sheet off her. He saw she was crying, he took the washcloth and wiped her buttocks where the blood had dried. Then he gently washed and dried between her thighs. He then covered her back up with the sheet and blanket. He could tell she was still crying by the movement under the blanket. She finally fell asleep.

He sat in the chair waiting for her to wake up, watching television to pass the time. Nikki finally started to stir, he then walked over and slowly pulled the sheet and blanket down. She lay stiff, afraid to move. As he laid down next to her, she started to shake.

“I won’t hurt you anymore.” He reached around her pulling her toward him, holding her firmly but gently.

“Please, go away, or just kill me.” She whispered.

He kissed her cheek. “I guess we’re on speaking terms again.”

He reached down between her legs. “Don’t!” She tried to say with some force, but the words barely came out of her mouth. She had no strength for resisting him.

He gently touched her, slowly stroking her in spots that he knew would feel best to her. She slowly responded physically, the natural reaction of her body to his touch. He knew she didn’t have complete control over that.

She felt him touching her and tried to resist becoming aroused, but her body betrayed her. She couldn’t resist much longer, what he was doing felt too good. She felt another part of her die as she opened her legs to let him have complete access to her.

He waited patiently for a sign from her. He could feel her getting moist, her folds of skin swelling as he caressed her, but she made no other movement or sounds. She would though, he knew she would. A few minutes later he felt her begin to move. She slowly moved her leg just enough to expose herself for him. He also felt the surrender of her soul to him once again, he smiled, kissed her cheek gently saying, "I want you, your mine." As he pushed his finger inside her.

He wanted this to be for her. He wanted her to feel pleasure from him so she would forget the pain. He listened as she moaned, he was aware of her breathing pattern and used it to bring her close to climaxing. He wanted to hold her orgasm off as long as he could, he wanted her to ask for it.

Nikki hated herself. She was welcoming his touch now, she felt him push his finger into her, and was glad he did. She was aroused and it felt good to her. He knew what he was doing, he had her to the point where she could no longer think, only feel what he was doing to her. She heard herself groan as he stopped right before she was going to climax. He changed the direction of his touch and repeated the same pattern twice more. This time as she felt herself near orgasm and him start to stop rubbing deep within her vagina, she pushed her pelvis toward his finger, and heard herself say. “Don’t stop… please!”

He continued to push and rub deep within her, and also rubbed her clitoris with his thumb. It only took a few seconds before she started to orgasm, she arched her back screaming as she did.

She felt him continue, it was wonderful. As he touched her clitoris she started to moan, all she wanted to do was cum. She never felt anything so wonderful, so pleasurable, she heard herself scream as her back arched almost on its own, it was the most fulfilling sexual experience she had ever had.

Once she finished she rolled over onto her side, facing Lobo, and wrapped her arms and legs around him. “Take me!” She said to his surprise. He did what she asked, he rolled on top of her remembering to give her pleasure and not take her for himself.

He rolled off of her when he finished and laid next to her, he pulled her toward him as he had done before. “I need you, Nikki. I thought I lost you.”

Nikki didn't answer him. As he pulled her to him it felt familiar, and comforting to her. She felt like she was his and that she belonged to him.

The next morning Lobo tried to remember what day it was. It took a few seconds for him to put it together so soon after waking. Monday, it was Monday the day the rest of the FBI agents were due to come back. As he lay in bed he knew it was time for him to make a decision about what to do next. He heard Nikki's phone buzz, he picked it up and read the message from Jessica. "Leaving now, will be there about two o'clock." He texted her back, "Okay, see you then."

He reached over and woke Nikki up. "It's Monday."

She turned her head to face him, she still found it hard to look directly into his eyes or even talk to him.

He stood up at the side of the bed. "I'm going to have to leave shortly. I need to know where this will leave us. Are you going to continue to track me down, or can I wait for you to come and be with me when things calm down."

Nikki was too traumatized to think straight. She turned away from him. “I can’t even face them right now! How can I?”

He really didn’t plan on any of this. His plan was to kill her, hide her body and disappear to another state long before the others ever even knew what he did. Instead he had gotten himself into this complicated tangle of a situation. He knew he had fallen in love with her. And now he would have to trust her, rely on her, and put his future in her hands. “She doesn’t even realize how much power she has over me!” He thought as he looked down on her lying in the bed.

He heard what she said. He wondered if she would be able to hold herself together. Maybe he should have killed her despite his attraction to her. It was too late for that now.

“I have to get a shower, then we’ll talk.” He walked to the bathroom worried about her. Maybe she wasn’t strong enough to do what he wanted her to.

After his shower he wiped the bathroom down everywhere he could remember touching. He dressed himself, and then using a damp washcloth wiped the other parts of the motel room down including the inside and outside of the doorknob. He picked up the key card and placed it into his pants pocket. Nikki had fallen back to sleep so she didn't see what he was doing, she wouldn't question him.

He sat down on the bed. Nikki started to stir feeling the bed move. "Nikki, are you going to be able to do this. Are you going to be able to face the other agents and act as if this never happened?"

"I don't know? I don't know? I can't bear the thought of seeing them, I've betrayed them! I would rather go with you, hide from them with you!" She said in a monotone voice with no real feeling in it.

He was getting frustrated with her, he picked her up by the arms. "Nikki, I need you to be strong, you have to do this. There is no other way! If I take you with me now, they will never stop looking for you. Do you understand that?"

Nikki started to put things together slowly. "Take me with you." She repeated his words.

"Yes, I would love nothing more. But it can't be right now. Once they stop looking for me then you can come and be with me. That's what you want isn't it?" He looked at her searching for a reaction. There wasn't much of a reaction from her for a few seconds.

"I don't want to be separated from you. How long will it be?"

She wasn't thinking straight. He could tell something was wrong. "Let's make a plan."

Nikki shook her head 'yes' as she waited to hear what he would say.

"You're not yourself and they're going to notice that. Therefore you're not going to be able to hide this weekend from them, are you?" He already knew the answer to his question. He laid her back onto the bed and sat on the side in disappointment. He reached into the drawer of the nightstand where he had put his knife and took it out. He held it in his hand and looked to see what time it was. They would be returning about two o'clock the message said. It was now one-thirty, she was not giving him many options.

"Nikki, you know you mean a lot to me don't you?"

"Yes." She answered with a smile on her face remembering that he said he wanted her to be with him.

"You need to trust me. I have a way for this to work out. It's the only way I know that will help you to face them when they get back here. If you're a victim, they won't question anything."

Listening to what he was saying made no sense to her. "A victim, a victim of what?"

"Me Nikki!" He said as he pushed his knife into her side. He heard her let out a scream, and try to pull away. He held her tight so he could do exactly as was needed, nothing more.

He pulled the knife from her and wiped her blood from the knife onto the sheet. Then he stood up and watched as she gasped, and writhed from the pain, he then turned and left the room. He knew the others would be back within a half hour. They would find her and take care of her.

She thought she heard the door, turning, fighting the pain in her side she looked for him. "He must have left, why did he do this? Where did he go?" She was unable to get up. She laid there waiting to die. She felt the blood oozing out of her when she put her hand over the wound he had inflicted on her.

It seemed like hours. She couldn't move. When she did the pain was too much. The stiller she remained the less painful it was. She thought of her family, and especially about her friend Stacey whom she believed she would soon see. She assumed she was going to die, that he decided to kill her after all. She lay waiting for the end to come.

CHARACTERS AND PLACES

Altoona, PA. = 2 hours south west of Wilkes-Barre. Where Lobo grew up, 3 ½ hours west of Allentown PA. Where the Oak Tree Land Development Corporation is located.

Amanda Westlake = 22 years old, roommate and best friend of Suzy Lamoy.

Bureau of Criminal Investigation = New York State Troopers who oversee cases requiring extensive investigation or involving felonies. These cases are referred to the Bureau of Criminal Investigation (BCI). The BCI is the plainclothes detective branch of the New York State Police. BCI investigators regularly assist local and county law enforcement agencies that lack the investigative resources needed for major crime investigations. Wayne Kemph, Sean Riley, Harry Greene, Gordon Bleaker, Greg Hines and Paul West.

Caesar = 2 year old search and rescue German shepherd.

Captain Hickory = Altoona police captain.

Charles = Loretta's husband, works in a factory as a shift supervisor.

Conservation Police Forest Rangers = Lester (Les) Snell, David Morgan and Luther Martin.

Daniel Dillon = FBI special agent in charge.

Dunkansville = South of Altoona, PA. Elizabeth's sister Loretta lives there on 8th St.

Elizabeth McMurray = Lobo's wife.

Francine Dapper = Technical expert at the FBI in Albany.

Frank Bronk, Sgt. = Worked the desk at the police station in Mackinaw.

Harry Mayfield = Husband of Jill who was hiking and saw Lobo in mountains.

Hawthorne Inn of Middletown = Where Lobo stayed.

Jessica Lewis = Part of NY State VCIT, also assists FBI team headed by Daniel Dillon.

Lobo = 5'8" black hair, blue eyes. Thirty four years old of Irish heritage (Lobo Ian Dylan).

Lobo Shaun Dylan = 55 years old. Father of Lobo. Lives on Beverly Blvd in Altoona, PA. Married to Josephine 53. Daughter is Kathleen who is 25 years old and married. Son is Collin who is 18 years old.

Loretta = Elizabeth's sister. Lives in Duncansville. Married with three children. Two boys 10, 8 and a girl 5.

Jack Sandler = Environmental Services Tech who saw Suzy as she left the hospital.

James Long = Threatened by Lobo when teenager.

Janelle Murphy = Captain in Wilkes-Barre police, lead investigator at the time of Nancy Walnick's murder.

Jason Newmann = VP at Oak Tree Land Development Corporation. 35 years old.

Jennifer Greyson = Reporter for Philadelphia Press who was following story of murdered Atlantic City woman.

Jerome McEvoy = Serial killer of 6 women New Mexico in 2002. Only caught because of car accident.

Jill Mayfield = Thirty something hiker who saw Lobo while hiking in mountains.

Jim Hershen = Nikki's partner in Mackinaw. Joined the army at 18, left after 10 years. Joined police force at 28. Now 37 he has been on the force for 9 years. He is married to his high school sweetheart, Laura. They have 2 sons, 17 year old James Jr. and 9 year old Devon.

John Rogers = Day manager at the Hawthorne Inn of Middletown.

John Sage = CEO of South Shore Memorial Hospital.

Johnson Smithers = PA coroner.

Judy Swansen = Local artist who sketched Lobo by description from desk clerk.

Justin Forest = FBI special agent, and partner of Daniel Dillon.

Kadi and Cindy = Worked with Suzy Lamoy. Cindy heard Suzy on phone with her sister Penny.

Knowlton = Town where Lobo and Elizabeth live close to. 20 miles NE of Wilkes-Barre.

Lamoy Family = Marshall 45 years old and Joanne 42 years old, Suzy's parents. Penny Lamoy 18 year old sister of Suzy, a senior in high school. 5'3" blonde hair, blue/green eyes.

Larry Enrish = Detective who investigated the Nancy Walnick case in Wilkes-Barre, works evening shift.

Larry Spruce = Captain of the Mackinaw Police. 55 years old, divorced. Married to his job. Slightly overweight.

Lawrence Mohar = Fake name Lobo used when called Jennifer Greyson at the Philadelphia Press.

Lindsey Gould = High school girl in Altoona, first girl Lobo killed. She was sixteen.

Mackinaw Village = Town where murder of Suzy Lamoy took place. Nikki's home town.

Mary Gurther = Thirty something hiker who saw Lobo while hiking in mountains.

Matt Newmann = 42 years old. CEO of Oak Tree Land Development Corporation. Married with 18 year old daughter.

Matthew Newmann = Retired CEO of Oak Tree Land Development Corporation. Retired 5 years earlier at 57.

Mark Gould = Deceased member of the Wilkes-Barre police who investigated the Nancy Walnick murder.

Maryanne Arbor = Clerk on duty at the Middletown Hawthorne Inn when Lobo checked out.

Mellany Short = 2nd body found who went missing in 2010 at 22 years old. Thought to have been near Albany/Troy area when disappeared. From New York City.

Middletown = 20 miles west of Mackinaw.

Milton Richmond = Chief of police in Atlantic City.

Mitch Doogan = Rookie, on the Mackinaw Police force for 1 ½ years.

Nancy Walnick = 2004 Wilkes-Barre PA victim who went missing Sept. 18, 2004.

Nikki Ardent = 28 and single. Independent rarely dates. Lives alone in a 2nd floor apartment in Mackinaw a small town in upstate NY. Works as a police officer in her home town for last 6 years.

Oak Tree Land Development Corporation = Located in Altoona. PA. Company Lobo works for.

Pennsylvania Locations = Allentown south east of Wilkes-Barre, Scranton 20 miles north of Wilkes-Barre, Knowlton twenty miles north west of Wilkes-Barre off route 6.

Robert Miller = Daniel Dillon's superior at the FBI.

Ronald Ardent = Nikki's father who left when Nikki was 8 years old. Was a police officer with English ancestry.

Ronald Jr. = Nikki's brother who is 27 years old. Is in the Navy and overseas most of the year. He is single.

Roseanne Ardent = Nikki's mother. Divorced, 57 years old. Minimum wage job at corner grocery store. Greek ancestry.

Suzanne = Nikki's 30 year old sister who is married with 2 daughters. 8 year old Samantha and 3 year old Emily.

Sam Archibald = Penny's boyfriend. Average 18 year old, born in November. 5' 7 light brown hair, blue eyes. **Maggie and Samuel Archibald** are his parents.

South Shore Memorial Hospital = On the south side of the Mackinaw Lake, outside of the town of Mackinaw.

Stacey Bernard = Missing friend of Nikki. Went missing at 20 years old on way home from work 8 years earlier. 5'5 blonde hair, blue eyes.

Suzy Lamoy = Victim. 22 years old, 5'4" blonde hair, blue eyes. Worked as a secretary on a medical floor at South Shore Memorial Hospital.

Violent Crime Investigation Team (VCIT) = Investigators Jessica Lewis, Mike Seagal, Roger Leary and Jason Deacon.

Headquartered in the New York State Police Forensic Investigation Center in Albany, New York, supports all law enforcement agencies.

Violent Crime Analysis Program (VICAP) = NYS VICAP is a computer-assisted program that operates in conjunction with the Federal Violent Criminal Apprehension Program (VICAP) administered by the Federal Bureau of Investigation.

Virginia Locations = Midlantic Inn was where Lobo was supposed to stay in Staunton, VA. Was supposed to search out land in Craigsville. Goshen, Raphine towns in VA where women disappeared.

9448562R00190

Made in the USA
San Bernardino, CA
17 March 2014